"I'm ⸻ the floor?"

"You want *me* to sleep there? Sweetheart, it was *you* who didn't listen to the warning about the burglar alarm. It was *you* who decided to knock on my bedroom door. However, I'll be a gentleman. The bed's king-size, so if we each keep to our own side there'll be plenty of room between us."

Kristin frowned at the four-poster and frowned at him. "And never the twain shall meet?"

"Got it in one," he said, and lay down again on the bed. "Don't worry, I'm not going to ravish you."

Anything can happen behind closed doors!

Do you dare find out…?

Over the following months, circumstances throw
four different couples together in a whirlwind of
unexpected attraction. Forced into each other's
company whether they like it or not, they're soon
in the grip of passion—and definitely *don't* want
to be disturbed!

Four of your favorite Presents™ authors have
explored this delicious fantasy in our sizzling,
sensual new miniseries DO NOT DISTURB!

Look out next month for:

#1996 **The Bridal Bed** by Helen Bianchin

ELIZABETH OLDFIELD

The Bedroom Incident

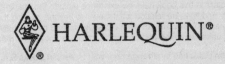

TORONTO • NEW YORK • LONDON
AMSTERDAM • PARIS • SYDNEY • HAMBURG
STOCKHOLM • ATHENS • TOKYO • MiLAN • MADRID
PRAGUE • WARSAW • BUDAPEST • AUCKLAND

ISBN 0-373-11994-1

THE BEDROOM INCIDENT

First North American Publication 1998.

Copyright © 1998 by Elizabeth Oldfield.

CHAPTER ONE

MATTHEW LINGARD rolled the tension from his shoulders, rested back in the soft leather seat and stretched out his long legs. Rain had begun to fall in yet another capricious April shower, so he would remain in his car until it cleared.

As he waited, he smiled. He had been offered a great opportunity—and faced one heck of a challenge—but he could do it. He knew he could do it. He was going to revamp the ailing *Ambassador*—a newspaper which the pundits had vowed was destined to 'corpse' before Christmas—fill a gap in the market and achieve rip-roaring success. Given time, dedication and, no doubt, a goodly amount of blood, sweat and tears.

Matthew watched the raindrops which spattered down on the windscreen. After two months of gathering and assessing information, making a thousand and one decisions and thinking, thinking, thinking, there were just ten days to go before the paper's relaunch. One outstanding item remained on his agenda: to find a replacement features editor. He released a weary breath. The features were a section of the paper which its new proprietor would insist on calling the women's pages...

Some time later—what seemed like an appreciably long time later—a voice coming through the partly open car window penetrated his consciousness. It was a decisive female voice.

'Sex is boring!'

Matthew yawned, blinked and struggled to come awake. He ground large fists into his eyes. There was no way he could agree with the statement, though had he heard right?

'It is. Sex is dullsville,' the voice declared, as if to provide him with personal confirmation.

Pushing back the sleeve of his jacket, he blearily inspected his stainless-steel watch. He muttered an oath. It had gone six. Returning his seat to its upright position, he looked out of the window. The rain had stopped, but the leaden grey clouds which hung low in the sky had created a premature twilight and the car park was murky.

Earlier his Aston Martin Volante had stood alone, but now an elderly Morris Minor was stopped several yards away. It had shiny resprayed purple bodywork, a beige canvas roof and a fluffy toy cat suctioned in a somewhat gymnastic pose to a side window. In front of the Morris, a tall, leggy, tawny-blonde in a cream wool trouser suit was pacing intently back and forth. She held a mobile phone close to her ear.

'Jo, I understand the attraction, but we've had so much that, frankly, I'm sick to death of it,' she said.

Lucky you, Matthew thought drily. It was a long time since he had made love. Far too long. He was thirty-seven, red-blooded and in his prime, yet he slept alone. But his career left him little time to devote to personal relationships. It had been the hours he spent at the newspaper offices which had riled his last girlfriend and brought about their split.

His brow furrowed. Be honest, he told himself. He had fast been losing interest and, in order to avoid a bombardment of inane chatter or being nagged, had stayed on at work later and later until the affair had simply expired.

'I don't care if everyone else does consider sex is an essential ingredient; for me it's become monotonous,' the young woman announced, grabbing back his attention. 'I reckon we should forget all about—'

Kristin broke off and stopped dead. She had thought the black low-slung sports car was empty, but now she saw a man with rumpled dark hair sitting in the driver's seat. He was looking at her, frowning and obviously listening in to her conversation. She glared at him through the gloom. Damned cheek!

'Jo, I must go. I'll talk to you again. Bye,' she said abruptly, and ended the call.

As she went to reach into her car to slide the phone back into her shoulder bag, the eavesdropper opened his door and climbed out. He stretched, long arms bent then reaching up. She eyed him stonily across the soft-top roof of the Morris. He was tall, broad-shouldered and well-built. He wore a grey corduroy sports jacket over an open-necked pale blue shirt, denims and trainers.

'I couldn't help overhearing,' he said.

'You couldn't have closed your window?' Kristin asked tartly.

He glanced down. 'Yes, I guess I could, but I didn't. Never thought.' He smiled. 'Will you please forgive me?'

His smile was lop-sided and his dark brows had slanted upwards in a small-boy appeal. She gazed coolly back. Whilst there seemed little doubt that most women would be turned to slobbering acquiescent mush, she refused to be so easily won over.

'If you use a mobile in public, you must expect people to listen,' he said. 'It's human nature.'

Kristin hesitated, then smiled back, relenting. His statement was true. 'You're forgiven.'

'Thanks,' Matthew said.

Her phone call had been intriguing. Whilst he accepted that appearances could deceive, there was something in the swing of her stride and her manner—like the way she had upbraided him just now—which spoke of spirit, zest and inner fire. She seemed eminently capable of passion. His eyes flickered down her slim, shapely figure. And was built accordingly.

Yet she had become bored with lovemaking? It was a sin and a shame. In his opinion, her boyfriend should not just be ousted post-haste, but deserved to be hung, drawn and quartered.

'In a recent survey of life's biggest irritations twenty-nine per cent reckoned it was folk talking on mobiles,' Kristin told him.

'That's a nice piece of useless information.'

She grinned. 'I'm full of it.'

'What was the biggest biggest irritation?' he enquired.

'Sixty-five per cent claimed junk mail.'

'I'd go along with that,' Matthew said, thinking of the charity pleas, double-glazing offers and cheap insurance proposals which landed almost daily on his mat. 'The ones I hate most are the letters which positively identify me as the mystery winner of ten million pounds.'

'But there's a catch.'

'Always,' he said, and turned to look beyond the visitors' car park and wet-slicked landscaped gardens to where a yellow sandstone castle rose up against the leaden sky.

'Are you here for the dinner this evening?'

'I am,' Kristin replied, following his gaze.

The castle was Flytes Keep, the home of Sir George Innes, a wealthy Scottish entrepreneur who had recently added ownership of *The Ambassador* to his portfolio of business interests. Built around an inner courtyard and surrounded by a moat, parts of the building dated from the fourteenth century. She smiled. With turrets, a drawbridge and comparatively small for a castle, Flytes Keep looked as if it came straight from the pages of a fairy tale.

'And I'm staying overnight,' she added, wondering if she sounded as amazed as she felt.

If anyone had told her, this time last week, that she would be interviewed for a fantastic new job and invited to stay at a private castle in Kent, she would have said they were nuts. But life was full of surprises.

'I believe everyone is,' he said.

'As it's Friday afternoon I had visions of getting snarled up in traffic and being late, so I left London early,' Kristin went on. 'Wadda y'know, the roads were clear.'

'Sod's law,' he remarked. 'And you put your foot down?'

'I tooled along the motorway at eighty.'

'You broke the speed limit? Tut-tut.'

Her hazel eyes sparkled. 'Didn't you?'

Matthew looked down at the thoroughbred vehicle which had purred along like a hungry tiger, eating up the miles. 'Once or twice.' He grinned. 'And then some.'

'So how long have you been here?' she enquired.

'I pulled in at around five, but on purpose because I wanted to speak to Sir George. However, when I arrived it was raining and as I didn't fancy getting wet I decided to wait in the car for a few minutes until it stopped. I closed my eyes and—'

'Zonk?'

'I was out for the count for over an hour.'

'You must've been tired,' Kristin said, her smile sympathetic.

He nodded. 'The past two months have been non-stop. Last week I decided to take a few days off and take things easy. I hoped to catch up on some sleep, but what with making notes until the early hours and Charlie creeping into my bed at the crack of dawn there wasn't much chance.'

'Charlie is your girlfriend, son, Labrador dog—who?' she asked.

'My nephew. I spent my so-called holiday with my sister and her husband and their son, Charlie, in Cheshire. I've driven down from there today. Charlie's six and a super kid, but—' he groaned '—he thinks I'm "cool" because I drive a sports car and he never left me alone. It was his Easter break from school and I was forever being inveigled into reading to him or going swimming or playing computer games until I damn near had double vision.'

Kristin laughed. 'I hate to be the bearer of bad news, but it'll get worse, I have a brother who's eight—a half-brother actually; my parents are divorced,' she said, and a fleeting shadow darkened her eyes. 'And when I stay I'm expected to take him and his friends on picnics and to collect frog spawn and to go roller-blading.'

He placed an anguished hand to his temple. 'Save me.'

'But you enjoyed being with Charlie?'

'I did. He told me that I'm his favourite uncle and although I'm his only uncle I almost burst with pride,' Matthew said, and paused.

He was not in the habit of regaling people with details from his private life—let alone such schmaltzy details—so why was he telling her all this?

'I'm going in now,' he said, becoming brisk. 'And you?'

Kristin checked her wristwatch. 'It's half an hour until my suggested arrival time so maybe—' she began hesitantly.

'You're going to sit alone in the car park twiddling your thumbs?' He shook his head. 'No.'

'No,' she agreed.

Matthew rolled up the window, removed the ignition key and shut the door. Opening the boot of his car, he lifted out a tan leather suitcase. The remote-control locking was activated and with a long stride which avoided a scattering of puddles left by the rain he walked over to the Morris.

The young woman was bent into the back. She held a couple of bulging plastic bags in one hand and was frowning at an assortment of others which, together with a dark green holdall, filled the rear seat.

'May I help?' he offered.

Kristin straightened to find her fellow guest standing beside her. She had already noted his broad brow, high cheekbones and strong features, but now she saw that his eyes were a clear blue, fringed with thick black lashes. He looked intelligent, self-assured and...steely. The kind of exciting, slightly dangerous stranger whom mothers were supposed to warn daughters about.

Her mouth curved. Job opportunity, visit to castle and now meeting Him of the Chiselled Jaw could be added to the list. There were ample reasons to be cheerful.

'Yes, please,' she said.

Chances were he would be working on the rejigged *Ambassador*, she thought as she bent into the car again, but in what capacity? Could his athletic physique indicate an interest in sports? Possible, and yet an inbuilt *gravitas* suggested he was a more serious journalist, perhaps specialising in politics or finance. Or did that steeliness mean he might be a war correspondent?

She lifted out two more carriers. Charlie's favourite uncle looked vaguely familiar. Had she seen his photograph somewhere, perhaps over a byline? That would explain the nagging feeling she had of recognition.

'Don't you own a suitcase?' Matthew enquired, taking the bags which she handed to him.

'Of course I do, but I wasn't aware until a couple of days ago that I'd be coming here and I've lent it to my flatmate, Beth, who's away in Greece. I know that marching into a place like Flytes Keep weighed down with plastic supermarket bags isn't exactly chic—' she made a face '—but I didn't have the inclination to fork out for a second case nor the spare cash.'

'No one's going to bother.'

'I'm bothered,' Kristin said, and felt a sudden twinge of nervousness.

The job for which she had been interviewed earlier in the week was not hers—not quite, not yet. But it offered a chance to prove herself which she desperately wanted and so she desperately wanted her stay at Flytes Keep to go smoothly.

'When I was packing I persuaded myself that the bags would look zany,' she told him, and sighed, 'but now—now I feel like a fool.'

'For no reason,' he said, with such calm certainty that she felt reassured.

Matthew watched as she continued to extract plastic carriers containing shoes, sweatshirts, magazines and unidentifiable silky feminine scraps.

'You've come well equipped for just one night,' he observed wryly.

'I wasn't sure what to wear and, when in doubt, I tend to bring almost everything.'

He lifted a brow. 'Only almost? You mean you've left the odd pair of wellingtons at home?'

'Plus some luminous lime-green flip-flops decorated with rubber bananas.'

'Big mistake.'

'Could be, but it's too late now.' She reached into the Morris to retrieve her holdall. 'That's the lot,' she said, turning to toss him a brilliant smile.

Matthew's fingers tightened around the handle of his suitcase. Her smile had sent a thought hurtling through his mind: You, I would like to take to bed. Perhaps it was because he had first heard her talking about sex, or because she looked so appealing, or both—but he felt a sudden desire. An outrageous desire which made him want to drop down his load, haul her into his arms and fiercely kiss that full, tempting mouth.

And if he made love to her he could guarantee that she would not be bored. Though maybe he was deceiving himself, he thought, a moment later. Maybe she possessed a low sex drive which rendered the poor girl unmoved—and unmovable.

'Did you put anything in the boot?' he enquired, his tone businesslike.

The urgent tweaking of his libido had surprised him. Whilst he had his fair share of testosterone and raging hormones, he was usually in control. He preferred to be in control. He was no longer a callow youth, excited by any passing pretty girl. He was a mature male, dammit.

'No. Or did I?'

Suddenly unsure, Kristin swung round towards the rear of the Morris, but then swung back. 'No,' she decided.

As she swivelled the second time, the heel of her cream suede ankle boot skidded sideways on the wet Tarmac. She gasped, tottered and, as if in slow motion, felt herself start to fall. The holdall see-sawed, plastic bags flailed in the air, and a bundle of black silk slithered out.

'Aaarrgh!' she cried.

Ditching his cargo, Matthew reached forward. He made a grab for her arm and caught hold, but, with knees bent, she was swaying back. She continued to tilt and as she fell, shedding bags and unstoppably capsizing, she tugged him off balance. He swore, half straightened and, somehow, managed to stand firm. Holding her upper arm, he gently lowered her the last short inevitable distance down to the ground.

'OK?' he asked as he let go and stood upright.

'No, I'm not. You big oaf!'

'I tried to save you,' he protested. Big oaf? He had expected her gratitude, not scathing condemnation. 'If I hadn't let you sit down, I'd have fallen down, too.' He frowned. 'And landed on top of you.'

'But you've sat me in a puddle!'

'A puddle?' He peered down and caught the glimmer of liquid. 'It's a very small puddle.'

Kristin felt the water soaking into the seat of her trousers. 'It's large enough to give me a sopping wet backside!'

'Oh, dear,' he said. 'The Goof Fairy strikes again.'

Her head jerked up. As well as the jokey comment, she had heard the rumble of amusement in his voice and now she saw that the corners of his mouth were twitching.

'I'm glad you find it so hilarious,' she said glacially.

Matthew readjusted his expression to one of sombre remorse. 'No, no,' he murmured.

'Garbage!'

'OK, maybe I do—a little.'

'A lot.'

'A lot,' he conceded. 'But you must agree—'

'I don't,' she snapped.

'I'm sorry,' he said, though he knew the words were useless. He held down a long-fingered hand. 'Grab hold.'

Tempted to haughtily refuse his offer, Kristin hesitated, but then she linked her fingers with his. In one fluid movement, he drew her upright.

'Thanks,' she said, stony-faced.

Sliding a hand into the hip pocket of his jeans, he pulled out a clean white handkerchief. 'Will you blot your rear end or—' the amusement was playing around his mouth again '—would you like me to do it?'

She froze him with a look. 'I can manage.'

As she got busy, Matthew gathered up the bundle of black silk from the ground and returned it to a bag. The bundle consisted of a lace-trimmed bra, suspender belt and pair of skimpy briefs. It was the kind of underwear of which fantasies were made. He could imagine the girl stretched out on white satin sheets with her long blonde hair spread loose across the pillow and the straps of the bra drooping—

Whoa, he told himself. After a year of celibacy, his hormones seemed to be kicking in with a vengeance.

'I bought this suit and my boots yesterday, specially for coming here,' Kristin said, mopping determinedly at her backside. 'The thrown-together look is usually my style, but I opted for a more professional image. Though now—' She lifted up her jacket and turned her back to him. 'How does it look?'

'Pert, well-rounded and infinitely pattable. You mean your trousers,' he went on, not missing a beat. 'They look fine and the water doesn't seem as if it's going to stain.'

She peered down. 'No, thank goodness.' She showed him his sodden handkerchief. 'What shall I do with this?'

'I'll have it,' he said, and pushed the handkerchief gingerly into his jacket pocket.

Taking a wad of tissues from her shoulder bag, Kristin continued to blot up the wet. She frowned. She had thought her companion looked familiar and, all of a sudden, she felt certain they had met before. Where? When?

She searched her mind. She sensed the meeting had hap-

pened a long time back, but why had they met? What was
the connection? A moment later the answer came...like a
punch which hit between the eyes. It had been in a London
restaurant, around ten years ago. She had been young, impetuous and in a state of high agitation—and he had been
her victim. She swallowed. A furious victim.

At that time he had worked for an up-market Sunday
newspaper as a whizkid deputy editor in charge of the colour supplement, so what position would he hold at *The
Ambassador*? Her stomach plunged. His calm air of confidence allied with the reference to wanting a word with Sir
George told her that he might be...easily could be...
probably was—the newly appointed editor.

'Are—are you Matthew Lingard?' she faltered.

'That's right.'

'The new head honcho of *The Ambassador*?' she asked,
needing to be doubly sure.

'Right again.'

Kristin balled the tissues in her fist. When she had so
publicly attacked him all those years ago she had not
known his name, but she knew it now. She also knew that
he was her prospective boss! Life *was* full of surprises, she
thought—good and bad.

She sneaked him a look from beneath her lashes. Him
putting her down, ever so carefully, slap bang into a puddle
had seemed like an accident, but might he have recognised
her and decided to get his own back? Matthew Lingard had
shown himself to be a tricky individual in the past, so the
idea was not too far-fetched. And if he bore a grudge she
needed to know. It was important she be aware of where
she stood with him right from the start.

Yet had he recognised her? He had shown no sign and
the girl who had rushed to the attack had looked very different from the young woman who faced him today.

'Did you do it on purpose?' Kristin asked warily.

'Do what?'

'Sit me in the water.'

He looked at her as if she had gone crazy. 'You're ac-
cusing me of putting you in the puddle deliberately? Lord,
no! What kind of a guy do you think I am?'

'Well, I—'

'A pretty mean one, obviously. I hadn't a clue the puddle
was there. It was behind you and I never saw it,' he said,
his voice harsh with indignation and his blue eyes glitter-
ing. 'OK, I smiled, but my sense of humour is not so
warped that I go around looking for ways of—'

'Calm down,' she appealed. 'I didn't mean to offend you.
It was just—' She moved her shoulders. 'I made a mistake.'

'You did,' he rasped. 'Believe me—' He stopped.
'What's your name?'

'Kristin Blake,' she told him, and waited.

Did he know her name from the past? Her full name?
Now that he had seen her again, would it ring bells? Her
stomach muscles clenched. Might he declare that there was
no way he would ever agree to employ such a wayward
creature?

'Believe me, Kristin, I'm sorry you got a wet backside
and I apologise again for finding it funny, but—'

'It was funny. Sort of,' she acknowledged wryly.

His anger evaporated and he grinned. 'Yep.' He picked
up his suitcase and his share of the plastic bags. 'When
you're ready—'

She retrieved her load and went with him.

As they walked between a pair of stone lions and onto
a path which led towards the castle drawbridge, she cast
her escort a sideways look. He had not recognised her from
the past and perhaps he never would. Their meeting might
have been dramatic, but it had been brief. A mere five
minutes.

Also, as the intervening years had altered him—his face
was leaner and he had crinkle lines at the corners of his
eyes—they had changed her. She had abandoned the close-
cropped elfin style and wore her hair long now. The addition of ten pounds in weight had transformed her figure

from stick-insect thin to shapely, plus she had gathered up a modicum of style, of poise.

Kristin grimaced. Though she would feel a darn sight more poised if plastic bags were not banging around her knees and her bottom was properly dry.

But if Matthew Lingard's memory should be jolted—well, the episode had happened in the dim and distant past and he would have dismissed it as—OK, embarrassing—but inconsequential. He obviously possessed a healthy sense of humour so, in retrospect, he would consider it funny. Wouldn't he? Yes. After all, it was her life which had been disrupted, not his. He would have also accepted that her action had been understandable and no more than he deserved.

She moistened her lips. Once she had been furiously angry with him, but now, whilst there were a few sparks of remembered resentment, she was prepared to let bygones be bygones. Time had healed and grievances had been mended. Besides, what had seemed like a disaster had, in fact, inspired a change of direction for which she was eternally grateful. She had forgiven him—and he would have forgiven her.

'Are you friendly with Emily?' Matthew enquired.

Sir George had told him he planned to ask some business associates to join the newspaper guests and said that Emily, his teenage daughter, would also be present. Kristin Blake's talk of a flatmate and—his eyes dipped to her left hand—lack of wedding ring indicated she was not a business wife, so he assumed she must have been invited to keep the girl company.

'Sorry? Oh, yes,' she said absently, and returned to her thoughts.

As Matthew Lingard had not recognised her name from the past, neither had he recognised her as a possible future member of his staff. At her interview, Sir George had explained the editor was away and yet she had thought that, in the meantime, he would have told him all about her in glowing terms.

Perhaps the proprietor had not wished to disturb his editor's holiday. Or perhaps Matthew had been told, but in the hustle-bustle of organising the new-style *Ambassador* he had forgotten. She looked at her escort again. Whilst he must be under all kinds of pressure, his lapse was not exactly flattering. Nor encouraging.

Kristin was wondering whether she should refer to her interview when a man in late middle age appeared from beneath the portcullis, followed by a youth who was pushing a luggage trolley. The man wore a black jacket, pinstriped trousers and starched white shirt. His thinning hair was brilliantined back, his carriage was stiff and his smile gracious. As he started towards them along the drawbridge, she felt a bubble of delight.

'Oh, gee,' she whispered. 'A butler.'

'You haven't come across a real live butler before?' Matthew enquired.

'Never.'

'It's a first for me, too,' he said, *sotto voce*, and their eyes met in shared amusement.

'But essential if you live in a castle,' she said, out of the corner of her mouth.

'As oxygen,' he declared.

'Miss, sir, may we take your bags?' the man said, in a plummy voice. 'Sir George is dealing with a business crisis and looks like being tied up for at least the next hour, but please allow me—Rimmer, the butler—to welcome you.'

Although it was generated mostly by nerves, Kristin needed to swallow down a rising giggle. As real Frenchmen often spoke and gesticulated like comic Frenchmen, and as Italian waiters invariably flirted, so he was the perfect English butler stereotype and beyond invention.

She slid her companion another glance and saw from the gleam in his eyes that he was thinking what she was thinking.

'Thank you,' she said, and was relieved when the youth stashed her plastic bags onto the trolley with as much solemn care and aplomb as if they had been a set of matching antique leather suitcases.

'Our pleasure, Miss Blake. I know you must be Miss Blake because Sir George described you in the most flattering terms,' the butler said, and smiled. He spoke to her companion. 'Good evening, Mr Lingard.'

'Good evening, Rimmer,' Matthew replied, and arched a brow. 'Sir George described me in flattering terms, too?'

The older man chuckled. 'What he said, sir, was that you were a tall, dark-haired gentleman who was bound to be wearing jeans.'

'Is there something wrong with jeans?' he enquired.

'Sir George considers them to be a little…casual, sir. Though that's only his view.' The butler turned to Kristin. 'What is your opinion, miss?'

'I think they're entirely acceptable so long as they're well-cut and—' she gave a wicked smile '—you have a pert and infinitely pattable backside, like Mr Lingard.'

Matthew burst out laughing. The retaliation was well-timed and he liked her sense of fun.

'The biter bit,' he said.

'Drinks will be served in the drawing room from seven-thirty, with dinner at eight-fifteen,' Rimmer informed them. 'Now if you would kindly follow me.'

Kristin turned, studying herself in the full length mirror. One of the perks of working for a women's magazine was that you came into contact with fashion designers who, on occasion, were willing to let you borrow a creation. So she was wearing a chocolate-brown satin evening dress with a scoop neck, narrow shoulder straps and lace panel down the back. Brown was, she had been gravely informed, the new black and a touch of lace was *de rigueur* this season.

She frowned at the curves of her breasts. Although the lace panel excluded the wearing of a bra, the bodice was as painstakingly engineered as a motorway bridge. Yet the neckline did dip alarmingly low—lower than anything she had ever worn before. Should she play safe and change into the white beaded tunic and palazzo pants which she had brought? Rimmer had advised that their host expected the ladies to dress for dinner.

Her reflection kicked out a high-heel-sandalled foot.

'Strut your funky stuff, baby,' it said, by way of a pep talk.

This evening she wanted to be visible and make an impact, and in this dress—boy, oh, boy—she would.

On being shown to her room, she had first unpacked. She had marvelled at the carved four-poster bed with its silver-pink drapes and matching coverlet, gazed out at the formal gardens and the rolling Kent countryside which unfurled beyond, then gone through to the luxurious *en-suite* bathroom.

Filling the tub, she had tipped in a generous helping of the lavender bath grains which were provided, stripped and carefully skewered her hair onto the top of her head. After enjoying a long soothing soak, she had dried herself, dressed and fashioned her hair into a sophisticated tawny twist.

Kristin headed back into the bathroom to fix her make-up. A bronze eyeshadow was finger-tipped onto her lids and a line of kohl applied. The more she thought about it, the more certain she felt that Sir George had not told his editor about her interview. And although he had assured her he would be delighted with his choice, he had also mentioned that Matthew Lingard had the final say.

She cast an anxious look at herself in the mirror. He would say yes to her appointment. Wouldn't he? He must. Her track record was good. She had shown herself to be imaginative and hard-working, and had enthusiastic references to prove it. The paper's proprietor had been impressed and, surely, Matthew would be impressed, too? She gave a decisive bob of her head. She was worrying unnecessarily.

She had always imagined her long-ago victim to be a cold, arrogant, loutish man, Kristin reflected, but he had seemed surprisingly warm and unassuming and pleasant. Wielding a wand of brown-black mascara, she brushed at her lashes. He was also a first-rate journalist. She could remember reading articles which he had written about politics and world events, and they were always a beat or two ahead of the others.

As she sprayed on a light floral perfume, her thoughts switched to her own writing. Before she went to join the other guests for drinks—and to wow Matthew Lingard—she wanted to jot down a few notes. Notes describing how it felt to be greeted by a butler, and about the excitement of staying in the splendour of a castle, and—she wrinkled her nose—about her plastic bags. She might never use the notes, but over the last few years scribbling down the events of her day had proved to be a worthwhile habit.

Standing beneath the jet of the high-velocity shower, Matthew massaged shampoo into his hair. He felt the thickness at the nape of his neck. He had meant to get his hair cut when he was up north, he thought ruefully, but he had not managed to find the time—thanks to Charlie.

As he rinsed away the bubbling foam, he frowned. Every time he saw his family—his parents also lived in Cheshire—he was faced with the same old demand. When was he going to settle down?

'You love Charlie, so why don't you get married and have kids of your own?' Susan, his sister, had asked, a couple of days ago. 'In a few years you'll be forty and then—'

Her shrug had indicated that once he reached the big Four-O he would be past his sell-by date. He did not agree. He ran a hand over his chest, down to the flat plane of his stomach and along a firm, muscled flank. He was in good shape and he planned to stay that way.

Switching off the water, he reached for a towel. He fully intended to marry, but it would be at a time of his choosing—which meant, as his career was currently so demanding and so absorbing, not for the next year or two. Or three.

Though he had yet to meet a woman who attracted him enough to want to love and live with her for the rest of his life. He had thought he was close on a couple of occasions, but had realised his mistake and sidestepped.

Matthew rubbed at the dark hair on his chest. Perhaps he was becoming choosy in his old age, but it was rare now that he met anyone he fancied, seriously fancied—though he had done today.

Dry, he ran a comb through his hair and walked back into the bedroom. Taking a pale pink shirt and a charcoal-grey suit from the wardrobe, he began to dress. When he met an attractive woman, he noticed the eyes first, then her breasts and next her legs.

Kristin Blake's eyes were large and light hazel, encircled with lush lashes. The breasts beneath the cream jacket had been high, not too small, not too heavy, and her legs were long. Add fine bone structure, the dusting of freckles over her nose, that wide, soft mouth and everything met his criteria. He had known more classically beautiful women, but there was a freshness about her—combined with a certain vulnerability—which stirred something inside him. She had been instantly and genuinely *likeable*.

Forget Kristin Blake and think about finding an editor for *The Ambassador's* features section, he told himself. He had hired a journalist whose work he admired, but she had discovered she was pregnant and had been forced to pull out at the last minute. However, he now had someone else in mind.

There was a knock at his door.

'Coming,' Matthew called and, pulling on his jacket, he went to answer it. He smiled. 'Good evening.'

His visitor was a short, conspicuously substantial man in his early sixties, with apple cheeks and a corona of grey hair. He wore a dark, rather old-fashioned three-piece suit with a snowy white shirt and gold watch chain.

'Good evening, Matt,' Sir George said, in his rolling Scottish accent. 'Sorry I was unable to welcome you, but there's a major breakdown at my bottling plant in Perthshire and the phone's been humming. Settled in OK?'

'Perfectly, thanks.'

'Did you enjoy your holiday?'

'Very much,' he said, ushering his visitor into the room. 'It's a while since I last saw my folks and it was good to see them again.'

'You should see them regularly. Families are what life is about, and all work and no play—' Sir George wagged a reproving finger. 'I wanted to have a wee word before we go into dinner. You know you need to recruit someone else to run the women's pages?'

Inwardly wincing at the phrase, Matthew nodded. 'I've been thinking about it,' he said. 'Have you heard of Angela Carr? She's a good solid journalist who's worked on several dailies in her time. She went freelance a while back, but—'

'I've interviewed someone,' Sir George cut in.

His brows lifted. 'You have?'

'Someone young, bright and with plenty of fizz.'

Matthew felt a stab of irritation. Before agreeing to take on the role of editor, he had made it clear that his acceptance would be on the strict understanding that he had full control over the editorial content of the paper—which included the hiring of staff. He had insisted he must be allowed to run things his way. He made the decisions, not the proprietor.

'I realise I was overstepping the mark,' the older man said, with a smile, 'but this is a special case and I won't do it again. I promise. I consider the young lady's ideal for the job and so will you.'

He was not so sure about that, he thought grimly. Sir George might have made a fortune out of bottling spring water, selling stationery, manufacturing industrial varnishes et cetera, but he knew damn-all about how to run a newspaper. And damn-all about journalists.

'What did you say to the woman?' Matthew enquired, wondering if a rash commitment might have been made.

In their dealings, the businessman had shown himself to be hard-headed, thoughtful and conservative, yet with the occasional flash of flamboyance. If his flamboyance had had him offering the job, the offer would be withdrawn, smartish. He refused to be landed with some 'fizzing' female.

'That you'd like her and you will.' Sir George shepherded him towards the door. 'I'll introduce you.'

'She's here?' he protested.

The dinner was a 'welcome on board' to the journalists who had been newly appointed and to those who were continuing on *The Ambassador's* staff. A muscle tightened in his jaw. The woman was not being welcomed on board. Far from it. Yet her presence signalled an expectation on Sir George's part and thus put pressure on him.

'I thought I'd keep her as a pleasant surprise. She's in the room next door to yours, though she may well have gone to the drawing room by now,' his host said, but as they stepped out onto the wide, thick-carpeted corridor he smiled. 'Perfect timing.'

Kristin slipped the key into her brown satin evening bag and turned. She had become so absorbed in making her notes that time had sped by and she had suddenly realised she was in danger of being late.

'Hello,' she said, surprised to find her host beaming at her from a few yards away.

Matthew Lingard was standing beside him, though his expression was grave.

'Kristin, I'd like to introduce Matthew Lingard,' Sir

George said. 'Matt, this is Kristin Blake, the young lady I interviewed for the women's pages.'

His smile was slight, without mirth. 'We've already met,' he said.

CHAPTER TWO

KRISTIN'S gaze travelled across walls of beautiful inlaid panelling, oil paintings and crystal chandeliers. Flytes Keep might be a castle with all the adornments of a stately home, yet it felt warm and lived in. A place of good vibrations. This was due to the bowls of fragrant white narcissi which were spread around, family photographs on the mantelpiece, but, most of all, to the easygoing affability of their host.

Her gaze stopped at the head of the long, white-damask-clothed table where Sir George laughed over a joke. In providing a delicious meal, permanently flowing drinks and giving the whole party overnight accommodation, he was a most generous host.

When inviting her, he had asked if she would care to bring a boyfriend along and she had said no; but the dozen or so business and newspaper men who were present this evening were accompanied by their wives or partners. Only Matthew Lingard and a man she had been introduced to as the arts editor, and whom she suspected could be gay, had come alone.

'Splendid wine. You need some more,' declared the man seated on her right, and before she could protest he gestured to a waiter who instantly stepped forward and refilled her glass.

The man ran one of Sir George's companies which manufactured industrial varnishes, and his name was Freddie. Earlier, as Matthew had told their host that they had met, a door had opened down the hallway and a middle-aged couple had stepped out. Sir George had introduced

them and had immediately been called away to the telephone—and Freddie had begun to chat.

He had dominated the conversation over drinks. Clearly
aware of this trait, his wife had taken the first opportunity
to drift away, then Matthew had excused himself and gone
to talk with members of his staff. Thus Kristin had been
left alone with the balding wordsmith, and it had seemed
impolite for her also to depart. She had hoped that when
the party moved into the dining room she would be able to
escape, but no such luck.

'We're sitting together!' Freddie had exclaimed delightedly, inspecting the place names.

Kristin took a sip of wine. An hour ago she had not
known industrial varnishes existed, yet after being told at
length about types, consistency and application she felt as
if she could pass examinations on the subject. But now, in
the pause after the main course of fresh poached salmon,
her companion had begun to regale a man sitting opposite
with the same numbing screed.

Freddie's enthusiasm meant she had barely managed to
exchange two words with Matthew Lingard, who was
seated on her left, let alone attempt to charm him. Though
as soon as they had taken their places a matronly brunette
who was on his other side had claimed his attention and
she had been talking to him—at him—ever since.

Kristin ran her fingers pensively up and down the stem
of her glass. The vibrations which came from Matthew
were not so good. He had plainly been shocked to discover
she was in line for a job on the newspaper—and his anger
was thinly veiled. But it was not her fault if Sir George had
kept quiet about her interview, she thought rebelliously.
Her brow crimped. Though it could be her problem.

'How long have you known Emily?' a low male voice
asked, and she turned to find that the subject of her thoughts
had been released from his verbal barracking, too.

She smiled. 'Since Wednesday.'

'Wednesday?' Matthew repeated, and frowned. He had

decided to do some probing to discover how serious the proprietor's promotion of Kristin Blake was likely to be—which would enable him to mount an appropriate offensive. 'But I thought you said the two of you were friends.'

Kristin looked along to the other end of the table where a dark-haired girl in a demure white broderie anglaise dress was chatting with guests. Chatting gamely, she noticed.

'I said I was friendly with her and I am. When we met at the interview on Wednesday—'

'Emily was there?' he enquired, in astonishment.

'Yes. She was eager to meet me—'

'Hang on,' Matthew instructed, cutting in again. 'If you didn't know his daughter, how come Sir George decided to interview you?'

'Serendipity.'

'You mean it was your lucky day at the job centre?' he asked sardonically.

'I mean he interviewed me because Emily reads my column, likes it and she'd suggested to him that I might be a suitable applicant for—'

'Emily suggested you?' he said, incredulity written all over his face.

'Correct. And when we met at the interview we immediately hit it off,' Kristin said, finally managing to complete at least one sentence.

'So this is what makes you a special case,' he muttered.

'Excuse me?'

'Which paper do you work for?' he enquired, lifting up his glass.

'I don't work for a newspaper, I work for *Trend*.'

'*T-Trend*?' he spluttered. He had taken a mouthful of wine and suddenly seemed in danger of choking.

'It's a women's magazine.'

Matthew swallowed. 'I know, I've seen it on the news-stands. *Trend*?' he repeated. 'Sweet mercy.'

Kristin's hackles rose. Typical male response, she thought. He was casually mocking her work—as it had been mocked by men before. She reminded herself of the hundreds of thousands of women who read and enjoyed the magazine, and tried not to care, but she did. The mockery hurt—and irritated.

Keep calm, she told herself. No matter how tempted you are to retaliate—and a high-heeled jab at his shins would be immensely satisfying—you want to charm him, so a smile has to be the wisest option.

'Poke fun if you must,' Kristin said, her tone light, then stopped as a young waitress appeared at her shoulder.

'Are you taking the pudding, miss, or the cheeseboard?' the girl enquired.

'Pudding, please,' she replied, and a cut-crystal dish of chocolate mousse in a coffee sauce was placed before her.

She eyed it with rueful delight, thinking of the calories it must contain and the extra miles she would need to cycle on the bike at the gym.

'For you, sir?'

'The cheeseboard,' Matthew said.

'Have you ever opened a copy of *Trend*?' Kristin enquired, after he had made his selection and the waitress had moved on.

'No.'

'Have you ever read anything I've written?'

'So far as I'm aware, I haven't had the pleasure.'

'Then why such knee-jerk horror?' she asked, with a smile.

He slung her an impatient look. 'Writing a column for a women's weekly magazine is a little different to running the features section of a national daily newspaper. A *quality* daily newspaper.'

'I do realise that.'

'Alleluia,' he muttered.

Her smile became forced. He did a good line in sarcasm.

'However, I don't just write a column,' she went on determinedly. 'I also—'

'I'm in the throes of offering the job to someone else,' Matthew declared.

He was bending the truth. He had yet to contact Angela Carr, but he would, he vowed, speak to her the minute he got back to London.

Kristin frowned. 'Sir George told me about the first woman you'd hired pulling out, but he never said another person had been approached.'

'Sir George didn't know. But—' his eyes met hers in a cool look which contained a warning '—I'm the one who makes the choices.'

'Obviously,' she murmured.

'Excuse me,' said a sandy-haired man who was sitting across from them, 'but did I hear you say you work on *Trend* magazine?'

Kristin nodded. 'That's right.'

As they had taken their seats, the man had introduced himself to her as 'getting ready to head the foreign news desk'. She had smiled, said her name, and been claimed by the garrulous Freddie again.

'My wife reads *Trend*,' he said, indicating a bespectacled woman further down the table. 'She reckons it's a cut above the other weeklies and there's a column in it which always has her chuckling. It describes events in the life of the writer, a rather madcap girl.' He grinned. 'That wouldn't be you?'

Kristin hesitated. Because she occasionally mentioned her family and did not wish them to be identified, she wrote under the initials KB. As far as the public at large were concerned, she was anonymous and she wanted to stay that way. She glanced at Matthew. Neither did she wish to be labelled in his mind as 'madcap'. But her questioner was another journalist and if she worked alongside him—*when* she worked alongside him—concealing the truth might be tricky.

'It is,' she acknowledged, then added, 'Though the column isn't always funny. I do write about serious matters.'

'Maybe, but I often hear chuckling. Hey, Bea,' he called, and his wife turned in their direction. 'This young lady writes the column in *Trend* that you think is so terrific.'

'You do?' the woman said, smiling. 'I just love your wicked streak.'

Matthew raised a thick dark brow. 'Wicked streak?' he enquired.

Kristin's heart sank. The couple were making her sound frivolous, wacky and faintly troublesome, but this was not the kind of image which she wanted to put across.

'When I was younger, much younger,' she emphasised, 'there was a time when I rebelled and went a lit- tle…haywire. I've referred to that period in my column.'

'Perhaps you'd tell me something I've always wanted to know,' said the bespectacled woman. 'Is everything which you write true?'

'Most of it,' she replied, 'though sometimes I use a little poetic licence to give an extra punch.'

'Like when?' the woman enquired.

'Well, for example, I once wrote about—'

As Kristin leaned forward to speak past him, Matthew was aware of the closeness of her body and smelled the faint fragrance of her perfume. His eyes followed the line of her profile—smooth brow, lightly freckled straight nose, determined chin—and travelled down the line of her throat to her bare shoulders. His gaze dipped deeper, to the neck- line of her dress where her breasts nestled as smooth and succulent as two ripe peaches.

She was the most striking woman in the room, he thought, by far. Know-it-all Freddie had spent the evening drooling and trying frantically to impress her, though she did not appear to have noticed.

'Was changing into a suit very painful?' Kristin en- quired.

Matthew's head shot up and, lifting his knife, he con- centrated on dissecting a piece of Brie. He had, he realised, been staring at her and could be accused of drooling, too. Had she noticed his interest? Heaven forbid!

'I beg your pardon?' he said.

'I wondered whether being unable to wear your Levis this evening had had you in tears?'

Matthew grinned. 'There was a slight watering of the eyes, but I gritted my teeth, stiffened my lip and sallied forth.'

'In style,' she said, thinking how dignified he looked in his charcoal-grey suit.

'You're looking pretty stylish yourself.'

'Thank you,' Kristin said, and took a belated mouthful of the chocolate mousse.

His grin, the first of the evening, together with the compliment, seemed to signify a softening of his mood which, in turn, seemed to offer an opportunity to tell him more about the asset he would gain by employing her.

'In addition to writing my column, I've been involved in many other aspects of the magazine,' she said, putting down her spoon. 'We run on a shoestring and everyone mucks in where needed, so I'm an all-rounder. I've compiled fashion pages, organised surveys, researched and written articles on such subjects as green issues, prison visiting, impotence.'

'Impotence?' he queried.

'I know all about it—' she tilted him a smile '—so if you require any advice?'

'Thanks,' Matthew said. 'I don't.'

'I've interviewed people from all walks of life.'

'Movie stars?'

She frowned. 'Yes, amongst others, though—'

'Whilst you may have gone down a storm with Sir George,' he said, 'I have my doubts about whether dishing the dirt on the latest screen idol fits you to be editor of *The Ambassador's* features section. We aim to be popular, but, like I said before, *The Ambassador* is a quality paper and it's my intention to maintain that quality.'

'Aren't you being just the weeniest bit stuffy?' Kristin enquired, restraining herself from stretching her vocabulary and saying something really impolite.

'Stuffy? Me? I'm not,' he protested.

'Yes, you are. People like to have an insight into what makes the rich and famous tick.'

'Maybe, but—'

'And you're being bloody-minded.' She shone him a smile which was somewhere between merry and murderous. 'I told you I write about serious subjects, but you ignore that and focus on movie stars instead.'

'Look, I'm sure you're very good at what you do,' Matthew said placatingly.

'You're patronising, too!' she flared.

'Stuffy, bloody-minded and patronising. If I ever need a character reference, I know where to come. However,' he carried on grittily, 'I shall have enough problems getting the new *Ambassador* off the ground without worrying about you messing up.'

'I won't mess up,' Kristin declared. 'I'm a professional.'

'So am I,' he shot back, 'and it wouldn't be professional of me to hire someone because their column happens to appeal to Sir George's teenage daughter. Anyway you'd be way out of your depth.'

Her hazel eyes flashed. 'How do you know? You don't. You have entirely the wrong perception of me, a perception which is based on complete and utter ignorance!'

Matthew swung a look around the table. The increasing heat of their exchange had started to turn heads and draw glances.

'We should drop this discussion,' he stated.

Kristin nodded and reined in her temper. It was not the time or the place to argue—and, indeed, she had never meant to argue. She had intended to be sweetness and light and to ooze charm, but he was so frustrating.

'For now,' she said.

She finished her pudding and a few minutes later their

host announced that coffee and liqueurs would be served in the drawing room. People began to move. As the mumsy brunette skewered Matthew in conversation again, Freddie sidled close. She gave a silent groan. A glint in his eye warned he intended to stick to her like glue for the rest of the evening and bore her rigid. And she wished he would stop ogling her breasts.

'Kristin!' someone called, and she looked round to see Emily waving and weaving her way towards her through the guests.

'I must go. Nice speaking to you. Please excuse me,' she rattled off, and swiftly made her exit.

'It's lovely to see you again,' Emily said, smiling and hugging her.

She hugged her back. 'And you.'

When they had met earlier in the week there had been an instant rapport and immediate friendship. The girl, who was shy and a little awkward, reminded her of how she had been at eighteen. An innocent, Kristin thought wryly.

'I wanted to sit near you at dinner,' Emily confided as they walked through to the drawing room, 'but Daddy's a stickler for protocol and he insisted I must act as hostess at the end of the table.' She turned down her mouth. 'I hate making polite conversation to strangers. Are you having coffee?'

'Please,' Kristin replied, and they went to help themselves from a buffet table.

At another table, waiters dispensed a selection of liqueurs.

Guests filled the drawing room, some sitting on the pale green couches which were strewn with silk oriental cushions, others admiring the paintings and sculptures, more standing together chatting.

'You were lucky, you sat next to Matthew Lingard,' Emily said, looking through the crowd to where the editor was talking to one of the newspapermen. 'I've never met him, but Daddy said I'd think he was a hunk and I do. He's gorgeous.' She sighed. 'He makes my toes curl.'

'Mine, too,' Kristin said, though her irony went unnoticed.

'Has he given you the all clear?'

She shook her head. 'We haven't had time to properly discuss my appointment.'

'I love the way his hair waves down to his collar,' the girl declared, gazing dreamily at Matthew as they continued to drink their coffees.

'It needs cutting,' Kristin said.

'I think it makes him look dashing and romantic, like a pirate,' Emily said, and giggled. 'A Spanish pirate. Did you know he has some Spanish blood?'

'No.'

'Apparently one of his grandmothers came from Barcelona.' The girl eyed her idol again. 'Let's go and talk to him.'

'You go. I've talked to him enough already.'

'I don't like to go over on my own. Please, Kristin, come with me and introduce me. *Please*. Daddy's busy and I'm dying to meet him and this is the perfect chance and—'

'All right,' she agreed reluctantly.

She had decided it would be wise to steer clear of the editor for the remainder of the evening. A tactical withdrawal would allow him to cool down, rethink and realise how prejudiced he was being. It would also enable her to adopt a resolutely less inflammable manner.

Kristin frowned. Even if he did have someone else in mind to head the features section, she was not about to give up. Not yet. She had been offered a chance to become a mainstream journalist and it was a chance which she intended to cling onto, albeit by her fingertips.

Dispensing with their coffee cups, she and Emily cut a path between the groups of laughing, talking people. As they approached, Matthew and his companion abruptly broke off from their conversation and turned to greet them.

'Your father's told me how well you're doing at school. Congratulations,' Matthew said, introducing himself and shaking hands with Emily, who blushed scarlet.

'My name is Rob Talbot; I'm the about-to-be home news editor of *The Ambassador*,' said the other man, who had fair hair, a thick moustache and was in his mid-forties. 'I've come with Matt from his previous paper. We've been buddies for years.' He grinned at Kristin. 'You don't seem so madcap to me.'

She darted a sideways look at Matthew. 'I'm the soul of sanity,' she declared.

'I hear you've been giving boyo here a hard time. Good for you; most women go so weak at the knees it's "yes, sir, no, sir, three bags full, sir". Uh-uh, I'm being summoned,' Rob said, eyeing a plump blonde woman in another group who was beckoning to him. 'That's my other half so I'd better obey or I'll be in trouble. Hope to catch up with you both again. Bye.'

'Is the lady his wife?' Emily enquired as the home news editor disappeared.

'For the past twenty years,' Matthew said. 'Why?'

'There're a couple of newspapermen here who came with their "partners"' the girl said, lowering her voice and glancing round, 'and Daddy doesn't approve. Each time he was introduced to a "partner"—' she enclosed the word with breathless inverted commas '—he became uptight. I've told him he's stuck in a time warp, but he's very prim and proper about things like that.'

'So he wouldn't be thrilled if you decided to shack up with some dream man when you're older?' Matthew enquired, in a wryly teasing manner.

Emily giggled. 'He'd go bananas, though I suppose he just might accept it if he knew we were going to be married. Daddy doesn't approve of what he calls "philanderers" either,' she continued. 'Once he was all set to employ a man to run one of his companies, but then he discovered he, um—' she blushed again '—slept around, and the whole thing was off.' She paused. 'When are you going to talk to Kristin about her job?'

He stiffened. The position of features editor was not 'her job'. He objected to the assumption—and he resented the increasing feeling he had of being manoeuvred. He took a mouthful of brandy from the goblet which he held. But rather than offending Sir George by refusing outright to employ his protégée, perhaps he should pretend to consider the idea? It would be what was laughingly called diplomacy.

'I'll squeeze it in some time tomorrow. OK?' he said, and Kristin nodded.

'Emily, my sweet, can you spare a few minutes?' Sir George called, and they turned to see him smiling from the other side of the room.

The girl sighed. 'I'll be back,' she said, flashing a grin at Matthew, and sped away.

'You were complaining to Rob about me?' Kristin enquired.

He hesitated, slowly swirling the amber liquid in his glass. He could fudge, but she had asked a direct question so he would give her a direct answer.

'Yes.'

She frowned. This afternoon she had thought him relaxed and friendly—but not tonight. Whilst he had treated Emily with gentle consideration, he was becoming progressively more hostile towards her. It was no more Mr Nice Guy.

'I'm sorry to interfere with your game plan,' she said, with a smile. 'However, when the red mist clears—'

'You think I'm angry?'

'I know you're furious. But—'

'We'll deal with this in the morning. You can fill me in on your experience and if I should decide you're suitable—'

'You expect me to spend the night dreaming the impossible dream?' Kristin enquired.

'Excuse me?'

'Tomorrow, as a courtesy to Sir George, you intend to go through the motions of an interview. You'll say you will consider my application and in a few days' time you'll send me a letter announcing that, sorry, I don't quite meet your requirements.'

Raising his glass to his lips, Matthew took another slug of brandy. Whilst he admired a brain, and it helped if it was attractively packaged, Kristin Blake was proving to be a little too sharp for comfort.

'My job is to reverse the fortunes of *The Ambassador* and make it pay,' he said heavily. 'Not provide a free ride for someone whom Emily's taken a shine to.'

'You can't resist the pathetic fallacy,' she declared.

'Which is?'

'You think that because I'm blonde I must be a bimbo. An airhead who intends to busk it. I'm not.'

'One thing I do think,' he said, 'is that you're young to head the features section.'

'I think you're young to be the editor of a national daily newspaper,' Kristin responded. 'Most of them are in their fifties, whereas you—'

'I'm old enough.'

'Ditto. And, as we're talking age, one of the reasons why *The Ambassador* has become duller than a lawnmower manual is because many of its staff are as old as Methuselah, have been there for years and are set in a groove.'

'True,' Matthew agreed, 'though the worst offenders are being despatched into retirement with a golden handshake.'

She nodded. 'I know.'

'Sir George told you this at your interview?'

'No, I read it in the papers.' Kristin shone a sweet smile. 'This may come as a big surprise, but I do read the serious papers. I've read about you, too.'

'What about me?' he enquired.

His appointment and the restyling of *The Ambassador* had created a considerable amount of interest and he had been interviewed both by newspaper journalists and on television. His brow creased. Whilst he was keen to publicise the paper, he was not into the cult of personality. He preferred to keep his private life private and his fifteen minutes of fame had been enough.

'I read that you have a reputation for cool, shrewd judgement, clear focus and having a will of iron. Also that you're six foot four and live in a mansion block in Kensington. Plus I read how you're the ''Golden Catch of the Year''.' She looked him coolly up and down. 'Or so one of the more sensational tabloids bizarrely claimed.'

'You don't agree?' Matthew said, finding himself amused. 'No, you wouldn't. After all, I'm stuffy and bloody-minded and—'

He broke off to look towards the doorway of the room where Sir George was clapping his hands for attention.

'Someone has asked if they could hear something about the history of Flytes Keep and take a look around,' the businessman said, when the group fell silent. 'I'm happy to lead a conducted tour. Would anyone else care to come along?'

As hands were raised and there was a general chorus of 'Me, please' their host beamed. He was proud of his home and loved to show off its treasures.

'We are in what was originally called the Withdrawing Room,' he declared, starting on a talk which he had given many times before, 'because after eating the company withdrew to this room.'

Sir George talked about the portrait of a bewigged haughty-looking individual which hung over the fireplace where a log fire blazed and crackled, then gestured for the group to follow him out. As they set off *en masse* along the main hall, Emily returned to Kristin's side.

'See you later,' Matthew said, taking advantage of the chance to leave, and went ahead to join Rob and his wife.

If the circumstances had been different he would have enjoyed Kristin Blake's company—she had an appealing personality—but he was damned if he would be bamboozled into employing her.

'In the mid-seventeen hundreds the Flytes, the aristocratic owners, fell upon hard times and the house fell into disrepair,' Sir George stated, leading the way into the library which had walls of leather-bound books and stained-glass windows.

'Then, towards the end of the last century, a wealthy American trader bought it. He embarked on a programme of painstaking renovation which was continued by his son and grandson. A few years ago, the grandson died, a bachelor without an heir, and—' he smiled '—I became the new owner.'

'Did you need to do any work on the castle?' one of his guests enquired.

'I updated the central heating and put in a fire-fighting system and the computer-controlled burglar alarm. As you'll appreciate, many of the contents are extremely valuable.'

'I've just bought the latest *Trend* and your column reminded me of the good times I'd had with Mummy,' Emily whispered.

Absorbed in what her host was saying, Kristin glanced round. 'I beg your pardon?'

The girl put a hand on her arm, holding her still and letting others go by until they were at the tail-end of the group. Kristin looked wistfully ahead. She would have liked to hear more about the castle, but Emily seemed eager for her attention.

'You wrote of how you'd gone shopping with your mother. Mummy and I used to go shopping together and—'

As the tour of the house continued, Emily talked—first about how much she missed her mother who had died the previous year, then about Kristin's column—most of which she appeared to have committed to memory. The girl's interest in her work was flattering, she thought, and frowned at where Matthew Lingard's dark head was visible amongst the crowd. It made a sharp contrast to his attitude.

By the time Sir George delivered everyone back to the drawing room, it had gone eleven o'clock. Some guests accepted the offer of another drink, while others professed a readiness to turn in. Matthew, she noticed—she seemed to be continually aware of him—had begun to look weary. He and Rob were standing to one side, each nursing a last brandy and talking.

'At first I used to cry whenever I spoke to anyone about Mummy, but it's getting easier,' Emily said. 'Though I don't think Daddy will ever recover. They were very close. I remember how—'

As the girl reminisced about her parents' happiness, Kristin heard the words 'features section'. She cocked an ear. Once again, it seemed, Matthew was talking about the post which she so much wanted.

'Don't bust a gut,' she heard Rob protest. 'OK, Sir George likes her, but that doesn't mean you have to hire the woman.'

There was a pause during which Matthew, whose voice was lower and frustratingly inaudible, spoke, then his friend started up again.

'Matt, I'm sure you can rise to the task of finding some way to persuade her to exit, without any fuss and while keeping her sweet.'

Matthew said something which, again, she could not hear.

A moment or two later, the two men moved away.

Kristin cleaned off her eyeshadow in swift smooth strokes. For Matthew Lingard to have marked her down as useless without knowing anything about her or reading a word which she had written was unjust. Unreasonable. And so maddening! She had brought a stack of magazines with her which she had intended to show him at her interview, but she knew that when he 'squeezed her in' tomorrow he would leaf cursorily through.

Loosening the glossy twist of hair, she began to brush. The editor was in the room next door, so why didn't she slip along and deliver the magazines to him now? she thought suddenly. That would enable him to take a longer look at her column and a longer look might make him realise that she possessed credible writing talent.

The evening was a little late, but he would not be asleep. When she had left the party he had been waiting with other guests to say goodnight to their host, so chances were he had yet to get as far as shucking off his jacket.

Matthew squeezed a ribbon of white paste onto his toothbrush and began to clean his teeth. He had a clear vision of how he intended to run *The Ambassador*—the spectrum the paper would cover, the downfalls to be avoided, the qualities he required in his journalists—and the vision did not include Kristin Blake. She might be the proprietor's dream come true, but he had no place on his staff for an *enfant terrible* from a women's magazine.

Spitting into the basin, he brushed his teeth again. Even if she had possessed a writing history which merited serious attention, he would hesitate to hire her because, if he did, he would be allowing Sir George to set a precedent. A dangerous precedent. He would be sending out the message that, despite all his tough words about making the decisions, he was open to coercion. The proprietor might then attempt to impose his own rule. He swilled out his mouth with water. Over his dead body.

This was, of course, supposition. Whilst he had had many business meetings with Sir George when they had worked easily together, he did not know him well on a personal basis. He frowned. If he did, he would have a better idea of how the older man would react to him rejecting his protégée.

Walking into the bedroom, Matthew drew back the

covers on the four-poster and climbed into bed. How should he play tomorrow's interview? In saying she suspected he would 'go through the motions' before despatching a 'no, thanks' letter, Kristin had already called his bluff—so did he act as if he was intent on winning an Oscar, insist she might appeal and pretend to solemnly consider her application? Or did he turn her down flat?

There was a third option; he could ring Angela Carr first thing tomorrow morning, offer her the position, and present the interviewee—and Sir George—with a *fait accompli*.

He pushed back the covers. He was too warm. The redoubtable Mrs Carr had experience, contacts and journalistic know-how on her side, he mused, though Kristin Blake scored in one area. As Rob had pointed out, she was far easier on the eye.

He recalled how she had looked earlier—elegant and yet oh, so sexy. Her dress had clung to her body like a second skin and there had been no sign of what his sister referred to as VPL—visible panty line. Did that mean she had not been wearing any panties? He gazed up at the canopy of the four-poster. The thought of her naked beneath the dress—all smooth curves and silky skin—was disturbing. And exciting.

Matthew rolled onto his side. Damp down the hormones and go to sleep, he instructed himself.

He was stretching out a hand to switch off the bedside lamp when someone tapped quietly at his door. Who could this be? he wondered.

As he levered himself up from the bed, his mouth curved into a grin. Sir George must have decided to speak to him again, and this time he had come to say that he had recognised his error in attempting to push Kristin Blake his way and wanted to apologise. Thank the Lord!

But as he opened the door his grin died. His visitor was a slender blonde in a brown satin dress. Her hair swung in loose buttery strands around her shoulders and her face had been cleaned of make-up—though this gave her an earthier appeal.

'Sorry to disturb you,' Kristin said, speaking softly because she was wary of disturbing the other guests.

A muscle knotted and unknotted in his jaw. To be confronted by her when he had just been thinking about her— naked—seemed like a dirty trick. It made him feel caught out and wrong-footed.

'What do you want?' he asked brusquely.

'To see you for a moment, only a moment,' she replied.

She had expected him to be dressed, but all he wore was a pair of navy boxer shorts. As her gaze took in his naked torso and tall barefoot stance, her heart began to thud. Matthew Lingard looked very male, very sexy and very annoyed.

'You'd better come in,' he said.

Kristin hesitated for a second or two, then walked inside. Emily's mention of him having Spanish blood had surprised her. He was dark-haired, yet not *that* dark. But now she saw the olive tint of his skin and the curls of black hair which grew on his chest. All of a sudden, he seemed fiercely Latin.

'I just wanted to leave my c.v. and these copies of *Trend*,' she said, showing him the plastic bag which she carried. 'I'd like you to look at them.'

He muttered an oath. 'Now?'

'No, tomorrow morning when you wake up. My column is at the front of the magazine, a page or two after the "Contents".'

'Forget junk mail—you are fast becoming my biggest irritation,' Matthew said, and raked a tired hand back through his hair. 'Do you never give up?'

'One of the attributes of a good journalist is determination,' she declared, with a smile. Crossing to a chest of drawers, she lifted the magazines from the bag and began to sort through them. 'I realise you may not find time to read all the issues—'

'I won't,' he said curtly.

'But I'd be grateful if you'd look at this one and—'

As Kristin opened a magazine at the appropriate page and reached for another, he walked back to the four-poster.

'I'm worn out,' he said, and stretched out on top of the bed.

She looked rapidly through the magazines, opening and closing them until six of her columns were selected and set out, ready and waiting for his appraisal.

'They'll give you a good idea of my versatility,' she said, taking a couple of steps towards the bed. 'But please, would you bear in mind that I'm writing for a specific market? Which doesn't—'

She stopped mid-sentence. Matthew looked so strong and virile and so...bare that she was suddenly conscious of being alone with him in his bedroom in the still of the night. She felt abruptly aware of how sexy and *desirable* he was.

He yawned. 'Which doesn't what?' he asked.

'Which doesn't mean I can't write for a national newspaper,' she jabbered. 'I don't expect you to keel over with delight when you read my column—'

'Thank God.'

'But if you could take a little time to study it in the morning I'd be grateful.' Spinning round, Kristin marched to the door. 'Goodnight.'

'Stop!' he ordered as she reached out to press down on the handle.

She turned. 'Sorry?'

Leaping up from the bed, Matthew strode rapidly across the room to grab hold of her arm and draw her back from the door.

'You can't go,' he said. 'You mustn't leave.'

She looked at him, puzzled. What was he talking about? Why the abrupt wish to detain her? Might he have had second thoughts about offering her the post of features editor? Or could he, too, have become aware of them being alone together and felt an urge to do something about it?

She might annoy the hell out of him, but she knew he found her attractive. Trouble was, it worked both ways.

If he did decide to do something—to kiss her—how would she react? she wondered. Would she find the strength to resist?

'Why not?' Kristin asked warily.

'Because it's gone twelve.'

'So?'

'The burglar alarm's been activated. When Sir George was showing us through the house, he explained that it's switched on from midnight through to seven a.m. Remember?' he said, his voice impatient.

'No.'

'You must.'

She shone a rueful smile. 'I think Emily might've been talking to me at the time.'

Matthew nodded. 'I noticed her yattering away. Sir George said that if, for any reason, anyone wanted to leave their room between midnight and seven they had to phone through to the security guard and ask him to override the system. He also mentioned that the last couple of times the guard has had to do that there's been a fault in the computer which has set off the alarm bells throughout the house.'

She looked at him. 'So do we phone the guard?'

'And risk the bells ringing and waking up everyone else? It's your decision.'

'If people were woken up,' Kristin said, frowning, 'we'd also risk letting them know that I was in your room.'

'Which is open to misconception,' he said drily.

'What shall we do?'

'What shall *you* do,' he corrected her, and yawned. 'I suggest you stay here until seven and then hightail it back to your own abode. Unless you have a better idea?'

She tried to think of one. 'I don't,' she said, and looked around. There was no couch or armchair in the room, only a stool which fitted beneath the dressing table. 'I'm supposed to sleep on the floor?'

'You want me to sleep there? Sweetheart, it was *you* who didn't listen to the warning about the burglar alarm. It was *you* who decided to knock on my door.' Crossing to the bed, Matthew lifted up a pillow. 'However, I'll be a gentleman.'

'No, you're exhausted. You sleep in the bed and I'll manage on—'

'An idea,' he cut in tersely. 'It's warm and I was going to sleep without any covers, so how'd it be if I sleep on top and you sleep underneath the sheet? The bed's king-sized, so if we each keep to our own side there'll be plenty of room between us.'

Kristin frowned at the four-poster and frowned at him. 'And never the twain shall meet?'

'Got it in one,' he said, and lay down again on the bed. 'Don't worry, I'm not going to ravish you.'

'I'm not worried, though if you did decide to try I'd scream blue murder.'

'I imagine you'd scream louder than the alarm bells,' he observed laconically.

'Right.' She glanced down. 'But what about my dress?'

'What about it?'

'If I sleep in it, it'll get creased. And it's borrowed and I have to return it to the designer on Monday and—'

'Take the damn thing off.'

'Think again, hon,' Kristin said drily.

'Look, as tempting as you are, you could—'

She shot him a wary look. 'I'm tempting?'

'You know it. I know it. However, as tempting as you are,' Matthew repeated, 'you could dance before me wearing only tassels in strategic places and I wouldn't respond. I'm too tired to do anything,' he mumbled, 'let alone be driven to a frenzy by...'

When his words trailed off and he yawned again, she crossed to the other side of the four-poster. She dithered for a moment, then crept in between the sheets. Although she did not want to sleep in the dress, neither was she willing to sleep naked. It seemed a little too much like living dangerously.

'I'm in,' she said, and he stretched out a long arm and, after some fumbling, switched off the light.

A minute or two later, Kristin heard the rhythmic sound of deep breathing which told her he was asleep. Tense and wide awake, she lay on her back. The chances of her ever sleeping with him stretched out beside her were minimal.

CHAPTER THREE

KRISTIN moved closer, closer to the firm male body. She was warm and half naked and in bed with a man. A lover. She knew she was dreaming and somewhere in the dim reaches of her mind a voice told her to enjoy the dream, to take it slow and easy and give herself up to each delicious moment—because it was rare she dreamed about making love.

Who was her lover? An actor of famed good looks? Someone she knew? A fantasy? She had a sense of a masterful man who was wildly attractive and wonderfully experienced in the intricacies of sex, but his identity was irrelevant. She felt safe with him, excited by him and all that mattered was his arm which lay around her waist and his masculine proximity. She snuggled even closer, wanting more.

Matthew stirred in his sleep. He was holding a woman, a warm, slender woman who smelled of summer flowers and who seemed to be wearing something slippery which had gathered up in folds around her waist. He desired her. It was a languorous desire. A desire which should be savoured and explored and which, when he finally thrust deep into the creamy depth of her body, would explode into endless rippling waves of sensual bliss.

He moved his arm from her waist, sliding it lazily up over the slipperiness which covered her ribcage until his fingers touched her breast. Her breast was naked. It was also firm and high and centred by a hard, silky-skinned nipple. He touched the nipple, feeling it quiver, and knew that, in time, he would kiss her flesh and taste. He would draw that succulent peak into his mouth.

Dreamily sighing, Kristin arched her back. Her lover was fondling her breast, his fingers trailing in a slow, sure, yet tantalising touch which made her skin tingle and was sending arrows of need feathering down to her thighs. She seemed to be melting, liquefying. She wanted him and he wanted her. She could feel the throb of urgency in his body and knew that, like her, he was caught in the tenderest moods of the soul.

As if in response to a wish she was barely conscious of herself, he shifted in the bed and his hands cupped both her breasts. She murmured her pleasure and her lover murmured something in return.

'Beautiful,' she thought he said.

Her eyes stayed closed, but slowly, slowly an idea wound its way up through the mists of her sweet intoxication. She had heard him speak, so she could not be dreaming. And the deep, mellifluous voice had belonged to...Matthew Lingard.

She ought to be shocked, Kristin thought hazily. But she wasn't. She ought to push away and climb out of the bed. She must. They were virtual strangers and the past had shown he could not be trusted. She would push away, she told herself, but as his fingers stroked desire overlapped intention, and won. Lost in a lethargic spell, her only focus was his touch. Such a wonderful touch which had created a shameless longing inside her.

Matthew drew in a ragged breath. The breasts beneath his hands were living flesh. This was not a dream. It was reality. A hot, reckless, heavenly reality. He struggled to think. Who...? Where...? Why...? As if drugged, he moved his palms over the taut nipples. God, they felt good. The woman felt good. The woman who was in his bed...who must be...Kristin Blake. Kristin who had had his sexual adrenalin pumping all yesterday evening and who was filling him now with a smouldering desire.

Although it went against common sense, against reason, he put his hand on her bottom. A man always paid for his mistakes, he thought vaguely. Problem was, her bottom was silky and sleek, and sometimes temptation was impossible to resist. Hell, he hadn't been to bed with a woman for ages and he was only human, he rationalised. He had needs. And if he kept his eyes closed he could pretend that his conscious self played no part in what was happening, bore no responsibility, and so could not be blamed.

'We shouldn't,' he heard her murmur, but she had begun to touch him, first stroking his back and then rubbing her fingertips over the coarse dark hair on his chest.

'No,' he agreed.

'But don't stop.'

'Can't stop,' he mumbled, and slithered his hand around to caress the smoothness of her thigh.

One thing was for sure, he thought: her sex drive was in full working order.

Kristin's breathing quickened. His mouth was close to hers. She could almost feel his kiss—the pressure of his lips, the moist twining of their tongues. She *needed* his kiss. She needed him. Moving her hand from his chest, she slid it over the flat plane of his stomach and down. As her fingers brushed against the hard organ beneath the cotton of his shorts, a quick heat jolted through her.

Matthew shuddered. He stroked the fuzz of soft hair which led to the intimate valley between her legs and touched her intimately. With a gasp, she arched up. He tenderly probed, seeking the moist invitation of her body, and she gasped again as desire burst and flooded inside her.

'Please,' she said, her fingers curling around the length of him.

'Yes.'

He knew what she was asking and it was what he needed. He needed them both to be naked—naked and free to indulge in a glorious exploration of bodies. He needed the freedom to touch every bare delicious inch of her and kiss and lick, and then thrust—

Brrriiinnnggg! Brrriiinnnggg!

The noise which shrilled out in what seemed a thousand raucous decibels beside their heads shot their eyes wide open and jerked them apart.

'What—?' Kristin asked, every nerve in her body twitching and twanging.

'Alarm clock,' Matthew said, and, rolling away from her, he reached out a long arm and switched off the clock which sat on the bedside table.

Silence.

He lay still—thinking, wondering, violently cursing himself.

She twisted the bodice of her dress around and pulled it over her breasts, then tugged down the skirt.

'What happened to you being the soul of sanity?' he demanded.

'What happened to your cool, shrewd judgement?' Kristin parried, and sat up.

She had been acting like a wanton brazen hussy. When her eyes had been shut she had not cared—she had revelled in every erotic minute!—but now misgivings were pouring in. How could she have allowed herself to be so unthinkingly and uninhibitedly carried away? she wondered. How could she have been so willing? It was absurd. She could not explain it—but he had encouraged her.

'You were supposed to be lying on top of the covers,' she said, deciding that attack was the best form of defence.

Right now, it seemed the *only* form of defence.

'You were supposed to sleep on your side of the bed, not creep over to mine,' Matthew retaliated, and pushed himself up, too. 'I must've felt cold in the night and come inside.'

'You don't remember?'

He jammed a pillow behind his back. 'I wasn't aware of it.'

'And were you aware of...touching me just now?' she enquired, climbing out of bed.

She had to put space between them. If there was to be

any hope of her reassembling even a shred of poise, it was vital she place him at a distance.

'Not at first. I thought I was dreaming and then—then I thought I was in bed with my girlfriend,' Matthew said defiantly.

He was not going to admit that he had known he was caressing her. How could he? It would make him look like a sexual opportunist and make a very difficult situation even worse. He had not felt as if he was taking advantage. Their lovemaking had just seemed to gather its own momentum and *she* had co-operated.

Kristin cast him a doubtful look. 'According to the "Golden Catch" article, you're not involved with anyone.'

'That's right, but I thought I was in bed with a girl I knew a while back. A long time ago,' he declared. 'I still think about her, often. I'll never forget her. She was so beautiful, with long dark hair and—' Stop it, he told himself. Not only are you lying through your teeth, but you're making the lie too complicated. He shrugged his shoulders. 'I haven't taken a vow of celibacy and everyone has their Achilles heel.'

'Only yours is higher up?'

'Funny,' he said.

'You may regard making love as an event which follows on automatically after dining with a woman, but I don't,' Kristin announced, desperate to try and claw back some dignity. 'I'm not into one-night stands. I think they're tacky.'

'Likewise. I've never gone for just sex.' Matthew gave a crooked smile. 'I'm too puritanical.'

'I would never've guessed,' she could not resist saying.

'I would never've guessed that you were sick to death of sex,' he responded. 'From where I was lying, you seemed amazingly eager.'

Her brow crinkled. 'What do you mean?'

'The way you wriggled close and stroked my chest and made a grab for my—'

'I was asking what makes you think that I'm sick to death of sex?' Kristin said, hot circles of colour burning on her cheeks.

She did not need him to spell out her behaviour; she could remember every explicit and embarrassing detail for herself. And yet, although she was awash with regrets, making love with him had felt so right…and so ecstatic.

'I heard you on your mobile yesterday. You were talking to Joe, your boyfriend.'

She shook her head. 'I was talking to Jo—Joanna Wells who is the editor of *Trend*. We were discussing future issues and she was saying how sex always sells and I said that, for me, the continual harping on about it in the media has become boring.'

Propped against the pillow, Matthew frowned up at her. 'I see,' he said.

'Take a look at the covers of women's magazines and there's almost always a headline which refers to sex. "Cash for Cuddles: women—and men—who marry for money",' she quoted. '"I Tamed a Hollywood Casanova".'

'"Knit your own Toy Boy"?' he suggested.

Kristin shone a quick grin. 'I like it. "My weeks of passion in the Arabian desert",' she continued.

'"How I slept with a guy whom I met less than twenty-four hours ago"?'

Yellow sparks flashed in her hazel eyes. 'Cheap shot. You were "amazingly eager", too.'

'I guess. But I am your average male and—' he let out a breath '—never underestimate the lust factor.'

Kristin shot him a look. A thought had suddenly occurred to her. 'You weren't…seducing me with the idea of persuading me to abandon my interest in the features editor job?' she enquired.

Pushing back the sheet, he climbed out of the four-poster. 'What the hell are you talking about?'

'Yesterday evening your friend Rob said he was sure you could find some way to get me to give up and bow out quietly, so you might've decided that a session in bed, followed by some smooth talking, would do the trick. As an alternative to spiking my wine with cyanide.'

'Now there's an idea,' Matthew remarked drily. He shook his head. 'I don't operate that way. Like I said, I thought I was in bed with a girlfriend and—' He broke off abruptly, to stride around the bed and face her. 'Perhaps seduction is—' he jabbed a finger '—*your* secret weapon in persuading me to employ you.'

'That's ridiculous!' she said.

'Is it? Consider this scenario: when you came to my room last night you knew the burglar alarm would soon be set and you timed your visit so that you'd be trapped. You were planning to have your wicked way with me then, only I spoiled things by falling asleep. But this morning—'

'This morning you put your arm around me,' Kristin said.

'And you moved in closer.' He fixed her with piercing blue eyes. 'On purpose?'

'You're suggesting that—that I'd sleep with someone in the hope of wangling myself a job?' she protested.

'It's been done before.'

'Not by me,' Kristin snapped, furious with him, but also angry with herself.

Although she had heard people talk of 'being carried away by lust', she had never imagined it could happen to her. She had believed she was much more disciplined and had far more sense. Yet their lovemaking had had nothing to do with sense, but everything to do with primitive forces and elemental need.

Matthew folded muscled arms across his chest. 'You're not a manipulative little madam?' he enquired, in a drawling laconic voice.

'No way!' she said, shooting the words out at him like bullets.

'Then how come Sir George is so fired up about you?'

'Are you insinuating that I've slept with him, too?'

He pursed his lips. 'No.'

'Thank you!'

'Though...' he went on slowly.

'Though what?' Kristin demanded.

'Though you might well be happy to exploit the fact that the guy so obviously likes you.'

'I do not exploit,' she snapped.

A dark brow arched. 'Is that so?'

'Yes, it is.' Infuriated by his disdain, she impetuously lifted a hand to slap his face. 'You, you—disbeliever!'

'Cool it,' Matthew instructed, catching hold of her wrist and deflecting the blow which she aimed with what seemed insolent ease. 'And keep your voice down; you'll be disturbing people.'

'Let me go!' Kristin demanded, but he ignored her.

'I apologise,' he said.

'So you damn well should!' she declared, tugging in vain to break his grasp.

Why must he touch her? It might be a prosaic restraining touch, but the feel of his fingers around her wrist had set her heartbeat racing. She felt an edgy, irrational desire. He was aware of it, too; she could see the charged emotion in his eyes.

'His daughter is the reason why Sir George is so "fired up", as you put it,' she said, her tone calm and matter-of-fact.

Matthew blinked. 'What?'

'Yesterday evening was the first time you'd met Emily, but if you'd seen her and her father together, just the two of them, you'd have realised that she's the apple of his eye. She was born relatively late in his life and is a much beloved only child. Apparently they were always close, but his wife dying last year has brought them even closer. Sir George takes great notice of whatever Emily says and he took note when she suggested me working on his paper.'

He stepped back, releasing her. Kristin had deliberately broken the mood, thank God. If she hadn't, he would have kissed her—out of anger, out of pent-up need—and they would have wound up making love. For sure. But after committing one error of judgement he had no wish to compound it with another. Or, to be exact, his head said no, though his body's urges were a different matter.

'So Emily is Sir George's weak spot,' he said, and could not help but be aware of how, unfortunately, Kristin Blake appeared to be his.

'You could put it that way.'

'And what makes her such a fan of yours?'

'She sees us as soul mates, because we're both only children and we've both been through...traumas. Apparently the first column of mine which she read was one where I'd described my emotions when my mother had walked out.'

'This was when your parents were divorced?'

Kristin nodded. 'I wrote about feeling sad and churned up and aggressive and guilty, but how I'd eventually come to terms with those emotions. Emily's mother had died a couple of months earlier and she said that, although the situation was different, it was as if I'd gone through what she was going through. She told me she'd cried and that reading the column had helped her.'

'It must've been difficult for you to write about something so personal,' Matthew said, frowning.

'It was,' she agreed, 'but it was also therapy. My mother and I had patched things up some years earlier and yet it was only after I'd written the piece that I truly forgave her. When Sir George's secretary rang to say he'd like to meet me, I hadn't a clue what he wanted,' she continued. 'And when I arrived at his office and he suggested I might be suitable for the features editor's position I was...stunned.'

'You didn't consider you were a suitable candidate?'

'If the job'd been advertised, I would never have applied,' Kristin said slowly.

'Ha!'

'However, sometimes fate takes a hand and—' she set

her shoulders in an unyielding line '—I know I can do the job and do it successfully.'

Matthew raised a brow. 'Is that so?'

'*Yes.* According to an article I read, when Sir George offered you the post of editor of *The Ambassador*, you were surprised. But you didn't turn your back on the opportunity, so why should I?'

He scowled. He could think of no answer to that.

'I know you feel I've been dumped on you,' Kristin continued, 'and I realise how I must sound—'

'Lightweight.'

'You don't pull any punches,' she said.

'Neither do you,' he replied, and they looked at each other in silent assessment.

'But you could at least give me a fair hearing,' she completed.

Matthew sighed. 'It's after seven a.m.,' he said. 'I suggest that you go.'

'I'm on my way and,' she added, with an arch look, 'may I suggest that you have a cold shower? Ice-cold.'

He smiled narrowly. 'I appreciate the advice.'

She was half out of the door when she turned. 'One last thing,' she said. 'I retract stuffy.'

As she walked along to her room, Kristin frowned down at her creased dress. She was thinking that when she got home she would need to wield a very careful iron, when she heard a noise behind her. She glanced back. Sir George was standing at the end of the hallway. He wore a grey sweatshirt and jogging pants, and was clearly on his way out for a run. Her heart sank. Caught in the act, she thought.

She stopped and turned to shine a cheery smile. 'Good morning,' she said, desperately ransacking her brain for something to say which would explain her presence and her appearance.

Her explanation had been impulsive and a little rash, Kristin thought ruefully as she stepped out of her dress a few minutes later. But acting on impulse seemed to be a part of her nature. It meant she had delivered the magazines at such a late hour and been forced to spend the night with Matthew Lingard. It had also had her confronting him in the past.

She sighed. Last night her aim had been gentle persuasion, but ten years ago she had demonstrated her disapproval. Demonstrated it in a dramatic—no, *melo*dramatic—fashion, she mused, her mind going back…

The seeds for her assault had been sown six months before she had ever set eyes on Matthew Lingard and a few weeks after she had left school for good. In an unusual, yet comically hackneyed episode she had been walking with a girlfriend through their local Surrey village when she was spotted by a woman from a model agency.

'What magnificent bone structure! And colouring! You have today's look,' the woman had declared, holding her still and inspecting her as though she were an entrant in a dog show. 'This is my card. You must join us.'

Her first reaction had been to giggle, as her girlfriend had giggled. Until not very long ago, she had tended towards the chubby and, whilst not an ugly duckling, she had believed her freckles made her cute rather than pretty. Never, in her wildest dreams, had she imagined herself as a model nor felt any inclination towards such a career, yet she had immediately enrolled with the agency.

She had been taught how to walk, introduced to fashion houses and, within weeks, was tripping up and down catwalks in London and Paris. Kristin wrinkled her nose at the memory. She had been eighteen, but a sheltered and naive eighteen.

When the other models had agreed to a photographer taking behind-the-scenes shots at a fashion show, she had agreed, too, she remembered. On the day in question, she had been so busy shedding one extravagant outfit and wriggling into the next that she had forgotten about the man's presence and had subsequently forgotten about the shots.

Walking into the bathroom, Kristin bundled her hair into a plastic cap and stepped beneath the shower.

A couple of weeks later, her father had been leafing through one of the top Sunday papers when he had suddenly thrust the colour supplement towards her.

'How could you do it?' he had demanded.

She had stared at a feature on the fashion show which included photographs in which she was undressing and, amongst non-nude pictures, showed her sometimes partially and sometimes completely bare-breasted.

'I didn't know the man was snapping me,' she had said, in dismay.

'Kristin, you must've done.'

'No, really—'

'It was another rebellion,' her father had declared, in an accusation which managed to mix sadness with disdain. 'But what will everyone think about my daughter exposing herself?' He had looked again at the photographs. 'It's like soft porn.'

She had frowned. As the headmaster of a select private school, her father was forever conscious of his position and wary of anything which might reflect badly.

'It isn't soft porn, Dad,' she had protested, and read rapidly through. 'The article is informative and matter-of-fact, and I'm sure no one's going to fuss.'

Kristin soaped herself down. Her teenage self had been wrong. People *had* fussed, in a variety of ways. The final straw had been when a reporter from one of the sleazier tabloid newspapers had turned up on the doorstep.

This had sent her hurtling into London to the photographer's studio. She had intended to start by telling him how underhand he was and carry on from there, but the photographer had been away on an assignment abroad.

'He took the more revealing shots for his private collection, dirty old geezer,' a trainee had said, when she had explained the reason for her visit. 'They were sent along in the batch by mistake and we were surprised when they appeared, but someone at the paper must've decided to print.' The youth had pulled a face. 'These posh papers may like to think themselves better than the rest, but they're not averse to showing the odd nipple or two.'

Determined that someone must pay for their sins, she had sped on to the newspaper offices and demanded to know who was responsible for selecting the photographs used in the Sunday colour supplement.

'The deputy editor,' she had been told by a receptionist in the appropriate department.

'I want to talk to him.'

'Sorry, he's out at lunch,' the girl had said, and mentioned a restaurant. 'It's a private lunch and we don't expect him back for a while.'

Rinsing off the soap, Kristin turned off the water and reached for a towel.

It was only when she had reached the restaurant that she'd realised she had forgotten to ask the man's name, she thought, replaying the scene in her head.

However, when she'd named the paper and nonchalantly claimed she was there to meet the deputy editor, a waiter had obligingly indicated a dark-haired young man who was sitting at a table with a debonair, affluent-looking man in his fifties and a soignée brunette.

As she had gazed at him, the brew of hurt, anger and resentment which simmered inside her had bubbled to the boil. He had selected and printed the photographs without her permission, without caring how she might feel, without bothering to think of any consequences. Forget the photographer, *he* was the true villain.

She had walked forward, Kristin remembered, and launched into a furious and somewhat garbled account of his sins. Then she had picked up a water jug, tipped it over his head, burst into tears and walked out.

The same day, she had informed the agency that her career as a model was over.

Padding back into the bedroom, she began to dress. The agency had insisted that she was foolish to miss out on future money, fame and glory, but it was one impulsive decision which she had never regretted.

CHAPTER FOUR

'You told Sir George what?' Matthew demanded.

'That we were engaged. Unofficially.'

He looked at her in horror. 'Are you determined to screw my life up entirely?'

'I'm not screwing anything up,' Kristin protested. 'On the contrary, I was—'

'What on earth possessed you to say that?'

It was three quarters of an hour later and they were in the dining room at Flytes Keep, helping themselves from a breakfast buffet of cereals, fresh fruit, stewed prunes, et cetera. Most of the other guests seemed to be sleeping in and the few who had appeared were sitting eating at the small tables which had replaced last night's long dinner table.

'Sir George saw me coming out of your room and looking, well, um—crumpled,' she began.

'You mean looking as if you'd just been "laid"?'

Kristin frowned and cast a quick glance around, checking that no one else could hear. 'Something like that. Anyhow it was obvious I'd spent the night with you and Emily had remarked on how prim and proper her father could be, so—'

'Engaged?' He shook a disbelieving head. 'Beneath that with-it exterior lurks an old-fashioned girl. You'll be telling me you're a virgin next.'

'I won't,' Kristin said.

'And Sir George believed you?'

She nodded. 'He seemed relieved to know that we'd made a commitment.'

'A commitment? After spending a single night together?'

'I said we knew each other from way back and had been—' she made an aimless gesture '—a couple.'

Matthew muttered an oath. 'Are you planning to put an announcement of our engagement in the Court and Social columns of the *Daily Telegraph*?' he enquired. 'Or do you prefer *The Times*?'

'I told him the engagement was *un*official,' she stressed, impatient with his sarcasm. 'I also explained that I was telling him in confidence and he promised not to talk about it to anyone else. Not even to Emily.'

'Let's be thankful for small mercies. You will promise to let me know when we're getting hitched? I'd hate to leave you waiting at the church.'

'Would you have preferred it if I'd said we'd been having a one-off roll in the hay?' Kristin demanded. 'Or that I was your live-in lover?'

His gaze travelled down her. This morning she wore a black V-neck sweater, plain tan skirt and tan boots. Her blonde hair was tied back in a simple ponytail. She looked clean, fresh and chic. Was she wearing the black silk underwear which had fallen out of her bag yesterday? he wondered.

'I'm not so sure about the live-in bit, but lover conjures up an interesting thought or two,' he said, his eyes snagging on hers. 'Though that is, in effect, what you've told Sir George.'

'How?'

'If we're merely talking about getting married at some indeterminate time in the future and we're sleeping together, then you are my lover.' His mouth tweaked. 'My fancy woman.'

'You might interpret such a situation in such a way, he doesn't,' Kristin said stiffly. 'Look, I spoke on the spur of the moment and to try and cover for you.'

'Cover for me?'

'If Sir George disapproves of "partners", then he's going to have a pretty low opinion of people spending a casual night together. Which is how it must've appeared. Maybe I overreacted, but I had a sudden vision of him sacking you—'

'No chance,' Matthew said firmly. 'I'm not a philanderer.'

'OK, but he might put a black mark against your morals and I assume you wouldn't want that.'

'No, though I could live with it,' he said, and added grudgingly, 'Thanks.' He eyed the pot of apricot yogurt which she held in her hand and his own bowl of muesli. 'Let's go and sit down.'

He directed her to a corner table, away from the others which were occupied. As they pulled out their chairs, a girl appeared to ask if they would like to order a cooked breakfast. They both refused, but requested rolls, marmalade and coffee.

'The idea of us being unofficially engaged doesn't thrill me, either,' Kristin said, when a basket of crusty bread rolls and a jug of hot coffee had been delivered and they were alone again. It had occurred to her that he might wonder if she had been indulging in some kind of wish fulfilment— and she wanted to squash the idea, fast. 'Firstly, you're not my type and secondly—'

'What is your type?' Matthew cut in.

'I like men who're sweet-natured and open-minded,' she told him, with a blithe smile. 'And, secondly, my mother married young and wound up divorced, and I don't intend to make the same mistake. Which means I shan't even think about matrimony until I'm well into my thirties.'

'And you're how old?'

'Twenty-eight.'

'Do you have a boyfriend who might suddenly appear and wreck your pretence?' he enquired.

She shook her head. 'The last guy was six months ago, but he became too serious too quickly and scared me off.'

'I know the feeling,' Matthew said drily. 'Did you live together?'

'No. I've never lived with a man. I had one serious relationship when it was discussed, but—' Kristin shrugged. 'Maybe I am old-fashioned, but to me setting up a home together for the first time seems to be part of the joy of marriage. But you've had live-in relationships?'

'A couple.'

Which I regret, he thought. At the time he had told himself the affairs were a run-up to marriage, but now he recognised that he had not been fully committed on either occasion.

Finishing his muesli, Matthew broke open a bread roll and spread it with butter and marmalade.

'By telling Sir George we were engaged, you were covering for yourself, too,' he observed.

She nodded. 'I wouldn't want him to think that I'm…flighty.' She ate a spoonful of yogurt. 'He wouldn't like the features editor of *The Ambassador* to be flighty, would he? OK, you haven't taken me on board—yet, but although the water may be choppy I am still afloat.'

'To mix up a few not very original clichés. Though you're not still afloat,' he said slowly. 'In fact, you've just pushed your feet into a pair of concrete boots.'

Kristin looked at him. 'What do you mean?'

'If Sir George believes we're engaged, I can hardly take you on as features editor. It wouldn't be ethical. I'd be open to charges of nepotism, favouritism and such.'

Her brow puckered. She had escaped one problem, but only, it seemed, to be faced with another. 'I didn't think about that,' she said.

'You could admit you'd made up the engagement story, otherwise—' he wafted a piece of marmaladed roll '—it looks as though you've put yourself out of the running.'

'To your great relief.'

For a moment Matthew wondered if he should attempt to deny the charge, then he nodded. 'This is nothing personal, but you have to see that if I appoint someone with zero knowledge of newspapers I'd be taking a risk.'

'So take a risk. Be daring, be different, live dangerously.'

'I already did, this morning,' he said, with a pungent inflexion, and looked beyond her. He raised a hand in greeting. 'Hi there.'

'Good morning,' Sir George replied, walking up to their table.

His jogging clothes had gone, replaced by a dark suit, regulation white shirt and the gold watch chain.

Kristin looked up at him and smiled. 'Did you enjoy your run?'

'Very much.' The businessman ruefully patted his stomach. 'I ought to go every day, but it's difficult to find the time. Why didn't you say at your interview that you already knew Matt?' he asked, pulling out a chair and sitting down beside her.

She hesitated, her mind whirling. She was not in the habit of telling lies, even white lies ad-lib, so should she own up to the truth? But explaining the truth—a censored version—promised to be difficult; and her earlier rumpled appearance meant that she might not be believed.

'We'd had a quarrel and broken up—oh, six or seven months ago, and I suppose it didn't seem relevant,' Matthew said.

She shot him a look of surprise. She had not expected him to make any comment; she had imagined he would sit tight and leave her to sweat. After all, whatever she said he seemed unlikely to suffer.

'Er—yes,' she agreed.

'But you met again yesterday and made up,' their host declared, beaming.

'We did,' Matthew replied.

Sir George's smile travelled between the two of them. 'You young people,' he said benignly.

'However,' Matthew went on, 'our renewed relationship means that unfortunately Kristin must withdraw her application for the post of features editor.' Reaching out, he gave

her hand what was clearly intended to be seen as a con-
soling squeeze. 'Isn't that right, babycakes?'

Kristin gritted her teeth. This, of course, was why he had
backed up her story. But his play-acting did not amuse her,
nor did his scarcely hidden delight at being let off the hook.
She also wished he would not hold her hand.

'Pull out?' Sir George said, before she could speak.
'Why?'

'Because if Kristin worked for me I'd be open to accusations of favouring her.'

'You wouldn't favour her. You'd never print something
which you didn't feel was up to standard, even if it was
the work of your fiancée,' the older man said. 'You'd put
the newspaper first.'

'Always,' Matthew agreed. 'However, other members of
the staff could decide I was slanted towards her and be
aggrieved.'

'Kristin said your engagement isn't common knowledge,
so I take it that no one at *The Ambassador* knows about
it?'

He frowned. 'That's correct.'

'So if you decide that she fits the bill you continue to
keep your relationship quiet. Then after a month or two,
when people have had time to realise there's no whiff of
favouritism, you can announce that you've fallen in love.
No one's going to object to an office romance. And hus-
band-and-wife teams can often work a treat.'

Letting go of her hand, Matthew sat back. 'Husband-and-
wife teams?' he repeated, in a strangled voice.

'When I started up my first company, my wife and I were
newly married and she was a tremendous help. She worked
in the office and gave me bags of moral support.' Sir
George sighed fondly at the memory. 'I don't doubt that
this young lady would be a tremendous help and support
to you.'

Kristin grinned. 'I'd do my very best. Babycakes,' she
added.

Matthew gave a taut smile. 'We only met up again yesterday,' he said, 'so perhaps we're rushing things. Who knows? It's possible we could have another row.'

Sir George stretched out a hand to pat him on the back. 'You're nervous of the idea of marriage? Don't be, it's a marvellous institution. Much better than all this living in sin. Phone calls to make,' he declared, rising to his feet. 'I'll see you later, Matt. In my study, in half an hour?'

He nodded. 'Yes, sir.'

'We might have another row?' Kristin said, when their host had disappeared. Her eyes sparkled. 'You can't mean that our engagement isn't going to last?'

'Not a minute longer than is necessary,' he said heavily.

'And here was I, thinking you worshipped the ground I walked on.'

'I'll let it ride for a while, so that we don't seem too fickle. Then I'll tell Sir George we've had second thoughts and you and I are over, kaput, a dead number.'

'What time do you want to "squeeze" me in this morning?' she enquired.

'I don't,' Matthew said.

She stared at him in dismay. 'You're refusing to interview me, despite what Sir George said about being at ease with our so-called engagement?' she protested, not sure whether she wanted to reach across the table, grab him by the shoulders and shake him—or bawl her eyes out.

'I'm not refusing, I'm delaying.'

She cast him a suspicious look. 'Oh, yes?'

'Yes. After I had a shower earlier—ice-cold, as recommended,' he said pithily, 'I went for a walk in the fresh air. I realised I'd been biased against you and that your application should be properly considered.'

'My soul runneth over with exuberant hope,' Kristin murmured.

'However, I haven't had an opportunity yet to look at your c.v. or the magazines and I shan't have time this morning. I'm also tied up pretty tight next week. But if you give me your phone number—'

'It's on my c.v.'

'Fine. I'll find a slot and call you.' Matthew gave a wry grin. 'Whatever my reservations, I figure you deserve a hearing if only because you're so damned determined.'

She smiled back into his blue eyes. 'Thanks.'

When he was being nice, he was very nice, she thought.

'I've never been sacked, though I did once lose a job which I was on the point of being offered,' he remarked as they drank their cups of coffee. 'It was a dream of a job, too.'

'Why did you lose it?' she enquired.

The contours of his face hardened. 'Because of some theatrical girl. I was lunching with my would-be employer and a girlfriend at a restaurant. We were discussing final details prior to my signing the contract and—'

'When was this?' Kristin asked guardedly.

'Around nine or ten years ago.'

She felt herself grow tense. 'And you still remember?'

'As if it were yesterday.' His cup clattered down onto his saucer. 'The girl threw wild accusations which killed any chance I had of getting the job and, coincidentally, ended my relationship with Mandy. If I could have got my hands on her, I'd have murdered—' He stopped to frown. 'Hold on,' he said.

She sat rigid. Matthew Lingard remembered. He had recognised her as the 'theatrical' girl. She had believed it was only her life which had been disrupted, Kristin reflected, but now it turned out that his had been altered, too. He had lost a dream job, thanks to *her*. There had been no forgiveness.

It did not matter that her accusations had been just; he had turned her into an enemy—with some reason. A cold finger drew an icy line down her spine. This meant he would refuse point-blank to interview her, let alone employ her, and could even spread the word around the newspaper fraternity advising she was to be avoided. Which would be goodbye to her hopes of becoming a serious journalist.

'Are you free tomorrow?' he demanded. 'Free for us to get together for an hour or so? Free to be interviewed?'

Kristin blinked. 'Um—yes. Any time.'

'Whereabouts do you live in London?'

'Notting Hill Gate.'

'Which is only a mile or so away from me. Suppose you come to my place at, say, eleven in the morning?' he suggested.

'I'll be there,' she said, and he gave her his address. She pushed back her chair. 'I'll go and pack my plastic bags and I'll see you tomorrow.'

'Until tomorrow,' Matthew said.

Kristin walked along Kensington High Street. Because it was a sunny day and she wanted some exercise, she had left her car at home. The shops on the High Street ranged from supermarkets to stores selling designer shoes, to high-fashion boutiques, to an indoor market where the stalls were piled high with black-fringed leather jackets much favoured by punks. Although it was Sunday, some of the shops were open and the pavements were busy.

By now Matthew would have read her c.v. and columns, so was he going to treat her as a credible candidate? she wondered as she swerved to avoid a girl handing out 'cheap hamburger' leaflets. Whilst he might have accepted that he had been biased, she knew that a major element in his agreeing to interview her was his wish to remain on good terms with Sir George. So would the morning be a charade?

Turning left, she went down a narrower side street and swung right into a garden square. Behind low railings, beds of bright yellow daffodils and pink tulips edged a green lawn. Plane trees cast dappled shade. On one side of the square was a small, white-domed church, while on the other three sides stood tall red-brick Victorian mansion blocks.

She located the building which housed Matthew's apartment, checked his number on the panel and buzzed. If he had not recognised her yesterday when he had been recalling the scene at the restaurant, it seemed unlikely he would recognise her at some later date, Kristin thought. The matter would not rear up and cause trouble. From that angle at least, she was safe.

'Hello?' His disembodied voice came over the intercom.

'It's Kristin Blake,' she said, her tone formal.

'Come on in,' he instructed. 'Take the lift. I'm on the third floor.'

As the small passenger lift ascended, she neatened the line of her jacket. This was a business meeting and she had dressed accordingly, in a smart navy skirt suit and white blouse. A wayward wisp of hair was tucked into the smooth knot at the back of her head. She intended to ignore her less than circumspect behaviour at Flytes Keep and guessed that Matthew would do so, too. Indeed, as an experienced man of the world he would have doubtless dismissed their intimacy as no great event. Her brow creased. She wished she could.

When the lift stopped, the door was pulled open.

'Oh, hello,' she said.

Matthew was waiting for her. Her pulse rate quickened. She had hoped she might discover he was not so attractive after all, but in a checked shirt and jeans which hugged his hips and emphasised his masculinity he was, as Emily had said, a hunk.

After greeting her, he directed her into the wide green-carpeted hall of his apartment and along to the living room.

'Coffee?' he asked.

'Thanks, that'd be good.'

'Have a seat. I won't be long,' he said, and disappeared.

Sitting in a green and white striped armchair, Kristin looked around. Whilst the furniture—sofa and two matching armchairs, a bureau, teak coffee table and a shelving unit—was stylish and of good quality, it looked sparse in the large room.

A watercolour of the Tower of London hung on one wall and books and piles of newspapers filled the unit, but there were no ornaments, no flowers, not even a pot plant. Nothing which brought the place alive. It was clear that her host devoted his energies to his career and used his home merely as somewhere to eat and sleep.

A few minutes later, he was back carrying two mugs of steaming coffee.

'Have you spoken to Sir George since we last met?' he enquired as he handed a mug to her.

'No. What would I speak to him about?'

Matthew levered his long body down onto the sofa. 'I wondered if you might've said I didn't seem too keen on employing you.'

'In the hope that he'd apply the thumb screws?' Kristin asked, a hint of tartness in her voice. 'Not my style.'

'Glad to hear it,' he said, and, putting on a pair of black-rimmed reading glasses, he picked up her curriculum vitae and started to scan through.

'I notice you gained top grades in your A levels,' he said. 'Didn't you think of going to university?'

'Yes, I did.' She took a sip of coffee. 'In fact, I was offered a place.'

'Where?' Matthew asked.

His manner was brisk and businesslike. On purpose. He had managed to persuade himself that the episode when he had almost made love to her—almost—had been a temporary madness, something to do with being sex-starved and half asleep. All right, now he knew that lust could attack like a dose of the flu, but it was over.

Yet when he had drawn back the lift door and seen her his thoughts had immediately flashed to how they had been in bed together. He had relived the feel, the warmth, the fragrance of her. And now an awareness of their intimacy floated like a spectre in the background.

'At Oxford, but—' she moved her shoulders in what was intended to be a casual shrug '—I decided against it.'

'Weren't your parents disappointed?'

'Yes, my father in particular. He's the headmaster at a boys' school, so for him academic success is important. He had great expectations, but—' Kristin shrugged again. 'After leaving school, I bummed around for a while,' she continued, being studiedly vague, 'then, as you can see, I took a secretarial course and got a job at the offices of a caravan and camping magazine.'

'You began as a shorthand typist, but soon became the editor's personal assistant and, in turn, joined their writing staff.'

'The magazine used freelance material and I wrote articles for them in my spare time. I'd never written before, but I discovered I loved writing. When more and more of my stuff was published, they decided I should be on the editorial team. I also had work published by other magazines.'

'Such as?' he enquired.

She reeled off a string of popular journals. 'Eventually I was head-hunted by the group which was setting up *Trend*. It's been going for four years now and circulation continues to grow.'

Matthew looked down at the pile of magazines which sat on the low table beside him. He had expected to read a bright, chatty, yet basically run-of-the-mill column, but instead had found himself reading quality work. OK, it was geared for the female magazine market, but it did not condescend. Just the opposite, it lifted. There was humour, nuggets of interesting information and plenty to exercise the reader's mind. She also had an ear for the things people thought, but rarely said.

'And your column plays a part in that,' he assessed.

'A sizeable part,' Kristin replied, deciding this was no time for false modesty.

'Why do you want to quit *Trend*?'

'Because I want to stretch myself.'

'Why not move on to another magazine? A monthly perhaps?'

'I want to work in newspapers,' she said.

'Why? What's the driving force behind that decision?'

Kristin took another mouthful of coffee. She had not expected him to grill her on her motives. 'Newspapers are
more immediate and more important.'

'OK, but who do you want to impress?'

'Why should I want to impress anyone?' she parried.

Matthew removed his glasses to fix her with serious eyes.
'It just struck me that—'

'Have you always wanted to be a newspaper editor?' she
enquired, needing to deflect him.

He grinned. 'No. When I was a kid I fancied being a
matador. I spent years waving a scarf in front of the cat
and giving it hell. I'd been taken to a bullfight and the guy
with the glittery suit made a big impression,' he explained.

'You were taken by your Spanish grandmother?'

'Yes.' His blue eyes narrowed. 'How did you know I
had a grandmother who came from Spain? I'm sure I didn't
tell any of the journalists.'

'Emily told me.'

'She seems to be big on the gossip,' he remarked.

Kristin smiled. ''Fraid so.'

'My father wrote political pieces for a northern paper,'
he continued, 'and, as I grew older, the idea of working in
newspapers began to appeal.'

'But you decided you'd prefer to be an editor, rather than
stick to writing?'

'Yes, though God knows why because basically it's a
maniac's job,' Matthew said, and frowned. He was supposed to be interviewing her, not her interviewing him.
'You understand there's a lot to do before the launch a
week Monday and that if you worked on *The Ambassador*
I'd need you to start tomorrow?'

She nodded. 'I've already spoken to my editor about it
and she's willing to release me. However, Jo wants me to

continue writing my column for a month or two, until she can find a replacement. It wouldn't encroach on my work for the paper,' she added hurriedly. 'I'd write the column at home. You wouldn't mind?'

He pursed his lips, considering. 'No.'

'I agree you'd be taking a risk with me, but safe can often be spelt D-U-L-L,' Kristin went on.

He gave a wry smile. 'You're not dull, but you are very tenacious.'

'You better believe it,' she said, and sat straighter. 'I have some ideas which I thought might be of interest for *The Ambassador*.'

'Like what?' Matthew asked, surprised to find her so prepared.

'Doing a series of interviews with politicians' wives, and looking into why people rush to appear on TV and reveal every last detail about their private lives.' She gave an impish grin. 'I'd also like to do something on the big unanswered question in biology.'

He lifted a brow. He had a strong suspicion he was being teased. 'Which is?'

'Why bother with men?'

'Oh, Lord,' he said, 'don't tell me you're a tub-thumping feminist, too?'

Kristin laughed, shaking her head. 'Not guilty. You may be negotiating with a journalist who, I'm sure, has vast experience in the newspaper industry,' she continued, becoming serious, 'but—'

'I'm not negotiating,' he cut in. 'I was economical with the *actualité*, as they say.'

'You are a prize rat,' she informed him. 'But you have someone in mind for the job?'

'Yes, though—' Matthew sighed and rose to his feet.

Walking across to the bay window, he gazed down at the square and the daffodils. He had rung Angela Carr that morning and received a cool response. She had doubts about *The Ambassador's* rebirth and was reluctant to risk being associated with its possible collapse. Hearing such negative remarks from a seasoned journalist had given his confidence a nasty whack.

He glanced over his shoulder at Kristin. Yesterday, as they had ended their meeting, Sir George had once again expressed his approval of her. He was keen she should be hired, but did that mean that if he refused the proprietor might insist? If so, was he prepared to *threaten* to resign? Or to *actually* resign?

No. He was damned if he would leave before his new job had got underway and, besides, any resignation threat should be saved for if a more important conflict arose. For example, a political standpoint. So did he employ her? Time was running alarmingly short and—

'Try me,' Kristin said, walking up beside him. 'I know you feel you're being press-ganged and I'm sorry, but if you don't try me you'll never know what you're missing.'

He turned to lift a brow. *'Double entendre?'* he asked, his mind going to the caresses which they had shared in bed and how agonisingly *close* they had been to making love.

She felt the glow of colour in her cheeks. 'I just want a chance to work for your paper.'

'You shall have one.' As she started into thanks, Matthew held up a silencing hand. 'It's on a temporary, three-month basis. If when the three months are through I decide you're cutting it, you stay on. If I think otherwise, it's farewell.'

'Three months isn't very long,' she demurred.

'Perhaps you'd prefer not to give up your job with *Trend* and take the risk?'

'Are you trying to discourage me?'

'No, I'm telling it as it is. I shall want to approve each idea, see an outline before you go ahead and read every piece which you and your team write,' he continued, 'prior to publication.'

'I'll be ring-fenced!' Kristin protested.

'I have to protect the paper and it's the deal I'm offering.'

'You're only offering the deal because you're not prepared to get into a fight and risk a bust-up with Sir George,' she said. 'Not at this stage.'

Matthew frowned. Was he so transparent? 'Perhaps. However—' He spread his hands in a 'take it or leave it' gesture.

She was silent, thinking. Whilst she did not relish his restrictions, she wanted the job—and to be offered it by *him* could be construed as sweet justice. He had printed the nude photos and demeaned her in her father's eyes—though her father had long ago accepted that she had not been to blame.

'Done,' Kristin said.

'Whilst *The Ambassador* will retain its broadsheet format, the aim in restyling is to fill the gap between the upper end of the tabloid market and the quality papers, and attract readers from both,' he said as they went to sit down again. 'The tricky part'll be getting the balance right.'

The clever part, she thought.

'Sir George calls the features the "women's pages"' Matthew carried on, grimacing at the phrase, 'and I agree that they should appeal to women.'

'Which is why you decided on a woman editor?'

'Yes, I believe a feminine viewpoint will be useful. However, I don't want an overly female slant, nor will I accept the kind of articles which would fit just as easily into a magazine. Whenever possible, the features should reflect something which is in the news *now* and, whether they deal with serious or lighter subjects, they must be entertaining.'

He went on to explain how she would be heading a three-strong team, then they discussed her salary and working hours.

'I assume no reference is to be made to our pretend engagement?' Kristin enquired as he ushered her out of his apartment half an hour later.

'Grief, no!' He sounded appalled. 'I don't want anyone at the office to hear about it. Or anyone else, for that matter.'

Her mouth curved. 'How about me gazing lovingly at you when Sir George is around? Or emitting the occasional sigh?'

'No, thanks. We keep everything between us matter-of-fact.'

'Yes, sir.'

'From now on, our relationship will be a working relationship. Pure and simple,' he said sternly. 'Is that clear?'

'As crystal,' she replied, and walked into the lift. 'Goodbye.'

As he went back inside, Matthew frowned. Who had he been telling? he wondered. Kristin—or himself?

CHAPTER FIVE

'A GLITCH-FREE launch,' Rob crowed, 'and so far every single comment anyone's made about *The Ambassador Mark 2* has been enthusiastic. What d'you bet when the audit bureau comes up with the circulation figures for this week they show another increase?'

'We've only been operating for a fortnight,' Matthew protested, 'and the new format is a novelty. OK, people are buying the paper, but that's because they're curious and who knows whether or not they'll continue to buy it?'

'You're too cautious.'

'I'm realistic.'

The older man shrugged, and looked at the clock on the wall. 'I'm off home. What about you?'

'Later.'

'Much later,' came the wry comment.

Matthew grinned, took off his reading glasses and rubbed his tired eyes. It was past eight p.m. and he had arrived at the crack of dawn. After a couple of quiet hours at his desk, the day had taken off like a runaway steamroller.

There had been the usual morning and afternoon conferences with his editors; he had had a meeting with Sir George and the company accountant, a session with the lawyer ironing out wrinkles from a possibly libellous article; he had dealt with a fusillade of phone calls from the Dockland works where the newspaper was printed. A problem had arisen which, after a long, nail-biting spell, had thankfully been overcome. And in between the meetings and the phone calls, he had overseen the putting together of tomorrow's edition.

'I guess,' he said, 'but this is my big opportunity and I don't intend to waste it.'

'You haven't got a wife to go home to, either; that makes a difference,' Rob declared. 'Y'know, it's time you thought about settling down.'

He groaned. 'Not you, too. My sister's forever nagging me to take a walk down the aisle.'

'How about walking down it with the appetising Kristin?' his friend suggested, looking out through the glass wall of the small office.

Matthew followed the direction of his gaze. Covering much of the second floor of the tall Hammersmith building, the general office stretched out in an open-plan maze of desks, flickering computer screens, shelves spilling with files—and figures; some people were sitting at their desks, others were scurrying around.

One of the figures, clad in a white polo-neck sweater and short beige skirt, and with her hair pulled back into a neat blonde braid, was his features editor. Looking sober and sensible, she was talking to a sub-editor who had recently arrived for the overnight shift.

'No, thanks,' he said.

'That was a bit sharp.'

'Rob, I don't have the time to be interested in her or in any other woman at the moment,' he said, softening his tone and smiling.

'Excuses, excuses. See you tomorrow,' his friend said, and went out of the door.

Sliding his glasses back onto his nose, Matthew began to read a report, just in, about the second day of a European conference on law and order. It was an important conference which would have wide-ranging repercussions and he planned to use it as a second lead story, but after a few lines his attention drifted.

Again, he looked out into the general office. The sub-editor, who was a fair-haired boyish young man, had placed his arm around Kristin's shoulders. When he gave her a quick hug and she laughed, he felt a searing blast of jealousy.

Matthew frowned. Why should he feel jealous? The hug was simple office camaraderie and, besides, he had no claim on her. Nor wanted a claim. In the three weeks Kristin had been working at *The Ambassador* their relationship had been strictly businesslike, strictly neutral—as he had stipulated. No reference had been made to the events at the castle. There were no 'you remember, I remember' looks. It was as if, by silent mutual agreement, their time together in bed had been scrubbed from the record.

Even so, he was paying for his mistake. His attitude towards her might be cool and official, yet whenever he looked at her he felt a whirl in his blood and a tormented sense of yearning. Whenever she smiled at him—and she had such a *gorgeous* smile—his heart seemed to spasm.

Why had he agreed to employ her, even for three months? he wondered, as he had wondered many times before. The decision was not rooted in journalistic logic, but had been partly to oblige Sir George, partly because Kristin had been so *eager* and partly due to an irrational twist in his nature which had made him want to keep her around. But he must be a glutton for punishment, he thought drily, for seeing her on a daily basis was provoking increasingly libidinous thoughts and inconvenient emotions.

Matthew shifted in his seat. He was at odds with himself about Kristin, but, thank goodness, he wouldn't be able to look out and see her for much longer.

Like the canteen, the boardroom and other rooms on the three floors of the tower block which the newspaper occupied, the editorial suite was being repainted, but it should be finished next week. So next week he would no longer be camping out in a glass cubicle with scratched furniture and scrappy rugs on the floor. Next week there would be no tawny-haired nymph forever at the edge of his vision, typing intently with the tip of her tongue protruding between her teeth, or flashing a long, slim leg or—

'Would you like something to eat, sir?'

Startled, Matthew jumped. 'Sorry?'

An office boy had opened his door and was speaking. Had he noticed him staring at Kristin? he wondered. He hoped not. Like all newspaper offices, this one was shaping up to be a hotbed of gossip. But he had no desire to be gossiped about by his staff.

'I did knock, sir. In about half an hour I'm going out to buy carry-outs, hamburgers and stuff, for some of the guys,' the boy went on, 'and I wondered whether you wanted—'

'No,' he said, shaking his head. 'I'll get something on my way home. But you could bring me a coffee from the machine. Black, no sugar.'

'Yes, sir.'

'Thanks,' he said and, determined to concentrate, he returned to the report of the conference.

Kristin put down the telephone, scribbled a note on her pad and peered through the increasingly patchwork activity of the general office to the editor's temporary quarters. Was he free? After a day when veritable hordes seemed to have tramped through his door, the answer was, surprisingly, yes.

Pushing back her chair, she got to her feet. As she began to make her way through the assembly of desks, she eyed his reading figure. She had expected Matthew to exhibit a ruthless, uncaring side at work, she reflected, as he had ruthlessly and uncaringly used her bare-breasted pictures. Yet his insistence that the paper should print the truth—which often meant political, commercial and personal misdemeanours—came accompanied by fair play.

She had also wondered if he might show an arrogance towards his staff. It was not so. Whilst he seemed to naturally command respect, his manner was easy and people liked him.

Kristin walked closer.

Although there was no doubt about Matthew occupying

the editorial chair, he had created a team spirit. His enthusiasm for turning the paper into a success was infectious; it flowed out and sucked everyone in. All the staff were motivated and rooting for *The Ambassador*—and for him.

Reaching his door, she knocked. The other editors tended to bowl straight inside, but as a new girl she did not want to appear too familiar.

'Come in,' Matthew instructed, his eyes fixed on the document he was reading.

Kristin entered the office and waited. She gazed down at his bowed dark head. His hair was cut in a shorter style than at Flytes Keep and it suited him. With spiky strands falling onto his brow, shirt sleeves rolled up above his elbows to reveal muscular forearms and wearing black-rimmed glasses which gave him a bookish air, he looked like... A tough professor, she decided. It was an intriguing combination. A sexy combination.

'What can I do for you?' he asked, abruptly whisking off his spectacles to look up at her with clear blue eyes beneath level black brows.

'Oh, um—' She blushed. She had been so engrossed in studying him that, to her confusion, she could not remember why she was there.

'Isn't it time you went home?' Matthew said, turning a broad hair-sprinkled wrist to inspect his watch.

'I am going, soon.' She managed to shake off her amnesia. 'But first I'd be grateful if you'd tell me what you think about my arranging for someone to interview Linus Boyd.'

'The pop star?'

'The same. His PR people have been on the phone to say he'll be in London for a concert next week and I could get one of my guys to see him.'

'Don't bother.'

Kristin frowned at the incisive command. 'Why not?'

'Are you arguing?' he enquired, with a dry smile.

'I don't argue. I have animated discussions,' she said. 'I interviewed Linus Boyd for *Trend*—'

'That's the first reason why not. Interviews with pop stars are essentially magazine fodder and, as I told you, magazine fodder is—' he slashed an olive-skinned hand '—out. The second reason is that many of our readers won't have a clue who Linus Boyd is and those who do won't particularly care.'

'But he's a pop star with a difference. He used to work at an old folks' home and—'

'Did he?' Matthew looked surprised. 'Even so, an article about the guy wouldn't tickle sufficient tastebuds.'

Kristin's temper sparked. For the past three weeks she had meekly gone along with all his decisions and obeyed all his instructions. She had not complained when he had insisted on examining every single features section lay-out which she had prepared. She had smiled when he had checked what seemed like every comma and full stop in pieces that she had written and done the same with the work of everyone else on her team. Yet it irked. She might be on probation, but she was not a complete novice and she resented being treated like one.

'You sound very sure about that,' she said, and was unable to keep the frostiness from her tone.

'An editor has to be sure.' Striding out from behind his desk, he opened wide his door. 'Bill,' he called, speaking to the lobby correspondent who, in overcoat and trilby, was making his way out of the general office. 'What do you know about Linus Boyd?'

'Who?'

'Linus Boyd—he's a pop star.'

'Never heard of him and couldn't give a damn. 'Night.'

'Goodnight,' Matthew replied. Closing the door, he folded his arms and leant back against it. 'Point taken?'

'If I may be so bold,' Kristin said, 'I would like to bring it to your attention that Bill happens to be middle-aged so he isn't likely to—'

'A fair proportion of our readers are middle-aged and for these first few weeks we have to tread carefully and make sure we don't bore them, don't lose them. I'm not saying a write-up about Linus Boyd wouldn't be interesting, perhaps in the Saturday supplement,' he said, relenting, 'but I reckon we should leave it for later when our readership is hooked. OK?'

'OK.' A beat went by. 'Point taken,' she added, seeing the sense in what he said and vowing to be smarter next time.

Matthew walked back towards his desk. It was the first time since her arrival that Kristin had questioned his word and the spat had had, he thought, a decidedly erotic frisson.

'Take a pew. You've fitted in here surprisingly well,' he said as she sat down. 'The past three weeks have been a crash course for you in the workings of a newspaper, but I'm full of admiration at the way you've coped.'

'You are?' Kristin said delightedly.

He nodded. 'You've had a lot to learn and plenty of stress—'

'Much of it from you,' she said pertly.

'I guess,' Matthew said, in wry acknowledgement. 'But you haven't been out of your depth.'

She smiled, feeling a rush of quite disproportionate elation at his pat on the head. 'Thanks.'

'I wondered whether some of the guys might kick up against working under a young woman who had no experience of newspapers,' he continued, 'but there haven't been any complaints.' His mind went to how the sub-editor had hugged her. 'On the contrary, you seem to have knocked 'em all bandy.'

'It's surprising what a short skirt will do,' she said casually.

And long legs, Matthew thought. Plus having that gorgeous smile and a natural sexuality which would melt a tank at fifty yards.

She flicked him a glance. 'You wouldn't fancy working under a woman?' she enquired.

'It depends on the woman and—' his blue eyes locked with hers '—on the work.'

Kristin felt something tighten inside her chest. For the past three weeks he had barely acknowledged that she *was* a woman, but he was acknowledging it now.

'You were right, a newspaper is a whole different ball-game to a magazine,' she said, in a determined veer. 'It's much more high-powered and I'm astonished by the amount of news which comes in. It never stops.'

'No, and yet at my last paper we once worked out that we only used around one per cent,' he said, and picked up the paper cup from his desk and swallowed.

'People in Britain drink twenty-two billion cups of coffee each year,' she said. 'How many cups a day do you drink?'

'Heaven knows,' Matthew said, and grimaced. 'That was cold.'

'Think of the caffeine and what all that coffee must be doing to the lining of your stomach. Yuck.'

'I don't smoke and I drink in moderation; I'm allowed some vices,' he protested.

'But you didn't have any lunch,' Kristin said.

'Lunch is for wimps,' he pronounced, with a grin.

'If you can't find time for a meal, you could eat a couple of apples. They provide fibre. But you had nothing.'

He slung her a look. 'You were keeping track of me?'

'No, I just…noticed.'

'And cared?' Matthew asked, and suddenly—and irra-tionally—found himself wanting her to care about him.

'I hate to think of the lining of anyone's stomach being ruined. What would your reaction be to an article on cos-metic surgery?' she went on swiftly.

He rested his hip on the edge of the desk. 'Too feminine.'

Kristin frowned. Wearing his usual jeans and sitting with his long legs spread wide, *he* was too masculine for her peace of mind.

'Men have their chins tucked these days,' she said.

'That's true,' he acknowledged.

'Would you mind if I asked for a second opinion?'

'Go ahead,' Matthew said, and when she went out into the general office he followed her.

She walked along to where the financial editor, a rather dour fifty-something individual, was riffling through papers on his desk.

'Would you read an article about plastic surgery?' she enquired.

The man nodded. 'See these?' he said, indicating the bags which hung beneath his eyes. He glanced around. 'This is just between the three of us, but I'm thinking of having them fixed.' He gave an unexpected smile. 'Then I shall be the spitting image of Tom Cruise.'

Matthew laughed. 'I think you're pushing it.'

'More like Richard Gere,' Kristin said.

The financial editor reached out to pat her hand. 'Thanks, angel.'

'Thank you,' she said, and looked at Matthew.

'OK, go for it. There's no need to start this minute,' he protested, when she crossed back to her desk, sat down and started to type.

'I just want to make a few notes.'

'Crazy lady,' he murmured, and moved away to answer a query from a sub-editor about how he wanted a story to be projected.

When the matter had been clarified, and a lay-out problem sorted, Matthew sat at a desk in the general office. He did this every evening in order to keep a closer eye on stories which had ended, on others which were continuing, on new ones coming in. First reports of a rail crash in the West Country had been received which, if the accident turned out to be serious, could mean a rearrangement of the front page above the fold.

'Go home,' he commanded, eventually walking back to where Kristin continued to type.

'In a few minutes.'

Taking a chip from a carton which sat on her desk, he put it in his mouth and chewed.

'You shouldn't eat these; they're bad for your figure,' he said, licking his fingers.

'And yours. Did it taste good?'

'Like ambrosia,' Matthew replied, for the chip had been hot, crisp and salty. And he was, he realised, ravenously hungry.

'So who cares about putting an extra half-inch on the hips? Live a little, that's my motto, for tomorrow you could walk under a bus.'

He smiled. Her down-to-earth attitude was refreshing. He had known women who were paranoid about adding an inch or a pound, and obsessive about what they ate. Or wouldn't eat. They made difficult companions.

'Mind if I have another?' he asked.

'Have them all,' Kristin said, thinking that there was something beguilingly intimate about him helping himself to her food. 'I've finished.'

As he ate the rest of the chips, he noticed a copy of *Trend* in her tote bag which sat beside her desk. Bending, he lifted it out and began to leaf through.

'It didn't happen like this,' he said suddenly.

'What didn't?' she asked, and looked up to see that he was reading her latest column.

It contained a humorous account of how she had been staying in the country and, loaded down with plastic bags, had bumped into a stranger in a car park.

'It was you who sat in the puddle, not me,' Matthew protested. 'It was you who got a soggy backside.'

She tilted her head. 'Are you going to sue?'

'No, but, grief, you make me sound like a real buffoon.'

'There's no reference to where or when, no names, so no one'll link it to you.'

'I guess not,' he said, and read on. 'What does t.d.h. mean?'

Kristin's stomach muscles clenched. She had not reckoned on him seeing the column. 'Tall, dark and handsome.'

'Aw, shucks,' he said.

'But you knew that.'

Matthew nodded, a grin creeping to his lips. 'Sure, though it was good to hear you spell it out.'

'I can get overly creative at times,' she declared. 'And I did wonder about adding "and slightly worn around the edges".'

'Slightly worn?' he protested.

'Don't worry, I like it when men have gone off a bit,' she said blithely. 'For me the saggy jowl and bulging paunch hold infinite charm.'

He chuckled. 'Build 'em up and knock 'em down.'

'I need to check something,' Kristin said, and, standing up from her chair, she speed-walked out of the office.

Since writing the column she had been working flat out at the newspaper and she could not remember exactly what she had written. But she needed to recall the phrasing, then she would be able to construct a defence. As she headed for the library, her brow furrowed. She had an unfortunate feeling she might have described how she had thought, Oooh, when she had first seen him up close or put in some other rash comment about how appealing he was.

Marching into the library, Kristin grabbed a book from the nearest shelf. It was obvious that she had been attracted—the bedroom incident could never have happened otherwise—but she did not want him to get the idea she might be seriously smitten. Even if she did spend too much time looking his way.

Air swished as the door behind her swung open and when she turned she saw Matthew walking in. Her nerves thrummed. His pursuit could only mean more teasing from him, which needed to be followed by quick put-downs from her—but her brain felt like porridge.

'Hello,' she said, cursing the impulse which had had her

writing about him. It was an error which would not be repeated.

'That should be a lot of help.'

'Excuse me?'

He indicated the book which she held in her hand. '*Swedish Blasting Techniques*,' he said, reading the title.

'Oh, yes. Wrong one,' Kristin declared, with a nonchalant shrug which disguised her tension. She stuffed the book back into its place. 'You know how you want the feature articles to tie in with current events whenever possible?' she said. 'And there's a law and order conference taking place?'

Matthew nodded. 'I was reading a report on it earlier.'

'How about an interview with Gully Knox, asking for his views on law and order? That'd tie in.'

'Beautifully.'

She smiled. The subject had been a diversionary tactic to keep any further remarks about her column at bay, but she was delighted that, at long last, he was giving straightforward agreement to one of her ideas.

'Right,' she said, 'first thing tomorrow I'll get busy and contact—'

'Not so fast.' Standing with his long legs apart, he hooked his thumbs into the pockets of his jeans. 'Are you suggesting that *you* interview a guy who, despite being found not guilty in court, is generally believed to have murdered his second wife and possibly the first?'

She had not got as far as thinking about who would do the interview, but now her chin took on a defiant slant. 'Why not? I've heard him on the radio and he's educated and articulate. His views'll make good copy.'

'True, but Gully Knox is also a wild card. He's anti-media and he threatened to knife the last reporter who cornered him.'

Kristin frowned. 'I didn't know that.'

'There's a lot you don't know.'

'But—'

'No.'

Her lips tightened. 'Just no?' she protested.

'As far as you attempting to corner the guy and interview him is concerned.'

'It'd be one heck of a scoop.'

'The scoop of the year,' Matthew said, 'but it'll never happen.'

'Suppose I can get Gully Knox to *agree* to meet me?'

A dark brow lifted. 'Now there's a radical thought.'

'Who dares wins,' she recited.

'He won't agree, so forget it.'

'If you're auditioning for the part of control-freak newspaper editor, the role is yours,' Kristin declared, her eyes ablaze.

She would, she decided furiously, find out where Gully Knox lived and write to him.

'Did you weigh into your boss at *Trend* like this?' Matthew enquired mildly.

'No, because she wasn't so damned annoying! She treated me as an equal, not a—a piece of fluff! I may be new to papers, but I'm not stupid and yet you double-check every t that I cross and every i that I dot,' she said, the grievances which had gathered over the past weeks bubbling up to the surface and bursting out of her. 'I'm thinking of enrolling for a course in primal screaming.'

'That bad, eh?'

'Worse! I want to become a respected mainstream journalist, but so long as you're calling every single shot I don't stand a chance!'

'Why are you complaining?' he asked. 'You like a man who has opinions, speaks his mind and is quite tough. A man to tangle with.' A smile inched its way across his mouth. 'That's what you put in your column and you were writing about me.'

'It was poetic licence,' she pronounced.

'You may fool some of the people,' Matthew said, 'but you don't fool me. And speaking of fooling—' He became serious. 'I didn't want to tell you this when there were flapping ears around and, I suspect, some who may lip-read, but I've told Sir George that we've broken off our engagement.'

'Already? That was quick.' Kristin slanted him a look. 'You didn't fancy me as your fiancée?'

'It was more the prospect of having to buy you a large diamond solitaire which I didn't fancy.'

'Skinflint, but I'd have settled for a small one. Or even zircons.'

Matthew bounced a hand off his head. 'Now you tell me. Will the ending of our betrothal have you sobbing into your pillow tonight?' he enquired.

'You flatter yourself,' she said smartly.

'You reckon?' Hooking a long arm around her waist, he drew her close. 'Funny, I got the impression you might be carrying a torch for me.'

'Horsefeathers—or some such word. Would you please let me go?' Kristin requested.

She had meant to issue a cool command, but her voice had come out an octave higher than she expected and changed it into a squeaky plea.

'Why? According to your column when we met there was, and I quote, "a hormonal buzz which could be heard in China" and I figure the population of Beijing'll be cocking their ears right now.'

She felt the clasp of his arm, the closeness of his body and the hammering of her heart. 'I don't know what you mean,' she said primly.

'Then I'll show you,' Matthew said, and he lowered his dark head and kissed her.

His mouth was firm and sure. It did not gently persuade, it unarguably possessed. She raised her hands to his chest, meaning to push away, but instead she surrendered—partly to his strength, but mainly to her own traitorous need. As she felt the touch of his tongue, her lips parted and the kiss deepened. Her arms slid up to wind around his neck. She melted against him.

How long the kiss lasted Kristin did not know, but when he eventually lifted his mouth from hers she felt light-headed and her legs weren't as steady as they might have been.

'Point taken?' Matthew enquired.

She gazed at him with bedazzled eyes. 'Uh-huh,' she said. It was the best she could do.

'So it's on again,' a rolling Scots voice declared behind them.

Like two clockwork soldiers, their heads jerked round, their arms fell to their sides and they stepped apart. Sir George was standing just inside the library door, smiling at them. One day a week, he left his company headquarters to the south of London and drove up to Hammersmith. Today was that day and, as Emily was away on a school field trip, he had stayed on late.

Matthew uttered a silent curse. Why did his boss have to come down from his office on the floor above at this particular moment? Why must he catch them out? But what had *he* been doing? He had meant to keep Kristin at a distance, not draw her into his arms.

Yet, whilst kissing her seemed like madness, deep down he accepted it as unavoidable. He had been plagued with a barely acknowledged need to discover whether his desire at Flytes Keep had been an aberration or if she would arouse him without the witchery of half-sleep and exotic surroundings. He frowned. Now he had his answer. She did.

'Wonderful,' Sir George proclaimed, seizing joyfully on the evidence which he believed they had presented. 'It's said that the path of true love rarely runs smoothly and you two are a match made in heaven. Sorry to interrupt,' he continued, 'but I came to find you, Matt, because I've been speaking to a friend who's the head of one of the television companies. They're keen to interview you, together with one of your editors, about the relaunching of *The Ambassador.*'

'When do they want to do it?' Matthew enquired.

'On their breakfast show, the day after tomorrow. I know you have morning meetings fixed with politicians and such over the next couple of weeks, but—'

'That morning is free,' he told him.

'Good. It'll be excellent publicity.' The proprietor grinned. 'You could take Kristin along with you.'

'No, thanks,' she said quickly.

Sir George's support was double-edged. Whilst it had been responsible for her being allowed a trial run at the newspaper, it had aroused Matthew's hostility. And now she did not want him to feel pushed into including her.

'Why not?' Matthew enquired.

Startled, she looked at him. 'You wouldn't mind?'

'I reckon it's a good idea. You know our aims and the gap we're intending to fill. You're enthusiastic. Have you been on television before?'

'Never.'

'Would you be happy to do it?'

Kristin nodded. 'So long as you brief me on the kind of thing you want me to say.'

'Then that's settled,' Sir George declared. Taking a slip of paper from an inside pocket, he handed it to Matthew. 'This is the number of the woman to contact at the studios. If your secretary gives her a call, she'll tell her where you're to be, when, fix a car, et cetera.' He smiled. 'Fly the flag.'

'We will,' Matthew assured him.

'Perhaps we can expect a public announcement soon?' the proprietor said, his eyes twinkling.

'About what?' he enquired.

'About the engagement,' Sir George said, and, after bidding them both goodnight, he walked out of the library.

'Hell and damnation!' Matthew said savagely.

'I didn't say a word, so you can't blame me this time.'

Kristin looked at him. 'But how come you didn't say a word, either?'

'Because I couldn't think how to explain. If it'd been the morning and I'd been fresh I might've managed to concoct some feasible story. But after a long hard day it was beyond me.' He ruffled his hair in an impatient gesture. 'So now we're back to square one. Great!'

She grinned. 'Impostors to Go.'

'You're taking it very lightly.'

'If I didn't laugh, I'd cry and that'd make a mess of my mascara. By the way,' she went on, 'I've changed my mind about settling for a small solitaire or zircons. I'd like a massive diamond. A knuckle-duster.'

Matthew gave a thin smile. 'Go home,' he said.

'Yes, sir.'

Although Kristin had agreed to depart when she returned to her desk she remembered a few more ideas for the cosmetic surgery article which needed to be noted. So it was another half an hour before she pulled on her jacket, collected up her tote bag and headed out through the office.

'Bye,' she said as she passed Matthew who was talking with the chief sub-editor.

'Bye,' he replied.

Outside, the night was dark. Tall streetlamps cast wide pools of white light, but in between the shadows were black. The cinemas, theatres and restaurants had yet to disgorge their customers and traffic was sporadic. The pavements were deserted.

Standing at the bus stop, Kristin looked back along the street in search of a red double-decker bus. No one else was waiting, so had she just missed one?

As she stood there, she noticed a man lolling in a shop doorway across the road. He had scruffy clothes, matted hair and he kept casting beetle-browed glances in her direction. He was probably only wondering whether to ask her for some spare change, but he made her conscious of being alone on the street and vulnerable.

At the sound of footsteps behind her, her nerves leapt and her imagination ran riot. Did the man have an accomplice? Was she about to be mugged? Her eyes wide and fearful, Kristin spun round.

'Matthew, it's you,' she said, smiling with relief.

Indeed, she felt so relieved and pleased to see him that it was all she could do not to throw her arms around his broad shoulders and hold on tight.

'I thought you came to work by car,' he said.

'I do, usually. But my flatmate had to go to Birmingham today and I've lent it to her. Are you walking home?'

He nodded. 'After spending so much time sat at a desk I like to stretch my legs.' He shot a glance at the figure in the doorway. 'I'll wait and see you onto the bus. Or why not get a taxi?'

'I will,' she agreed.

'About my being a control freak,' Matthew said as she looked down the street for a cab. 'Maybe I have gone a little over the top. As from now, you're allowed to use your own initiative.'

Kristin smiled. 'So if I'm rung up and offered an interview which I think will suit I can arrange it without asking your permission?'

He nodded. 'Though I shall want to check out the piece before it goes into the paper.'

'There is an interview which I reckon would tickle the tastebuds,' she said.

'Fix it. Surprise me. Here's a taxi,' he said, and flagged it down.

As the vehicle came to a stop beside them, Kristin told the driver her destination.

'This should cover it,' Matthew said, taking a note from his wallet and handing it to him.

'Thanks, but there's no need,' she began to protest.

'My treat,' he said, and bent forward to brush his lips against hers in a soft dry kiss which she found incredibly erotic.

'What—?' She needed to take a short quick breath in order to continue. 'What was that for?'

'We are supposed to be unofficially engaged again, so far as Sir George is concerned.' He opened the passenger door and ushered her inside. 'Remember?'

'As if I could ever forget,' Kristin said wryly.

'Goodnight.'

'Night,' she replied, and the taxi drew away.

CHAPTER SIX

KRISTIN had not needed to work long in journalism before she had realised that the venue which a celebrity chose for an interview could often be a blatant giveaway of character. Amanda Cousins, television's current 'it' girl, had said she would meet her for lunch at one of London's riverside restaurants. Smart and wallet-tremblingly expensive, the restaurant was famous as a place where the showbusiness glitterati went to see and to be seen.

As soon as the revolving doors had emptied her into the reception area, she had seen the TV presenter. Petite, raven-haired and clad in fondant-pink cashmere, floor-punching stilettos and dark glasses, she was curled up in the corner of a white leather sofa directly opposite.

'You're early,' Kristin had remarked, after introducing herself.

'And exhausted from signing so many autographs,' her guest had declared, with a gurgling laugh. 'Wherever I go, my fans always seem to find me.'

Which is not surprising if you sit where no one can possibly miss you, she had thought. And wear sunglasses indoors on an overcast day in May.

Though the designer sunglasses served a second purpose. At regular intervals, they were slid down the short straight nose to reveal a pair of astonishingly violet eyes fringed with luxuriant black lashes. The trick might have been well-rehearsed, but it was awesomely professional and always worked. Each time Kristin found herself fascinated—to her increasing exasperation.

As her guest's early arrival appeared to have been on purpose in order to indulge in some ego-massaging, so she suspected it had also enabled her to pre-select their table. After posing in the doorway to the dining room, Amanda had sashayed straight to a table which sat on a dais beside the window and was beneath a spotlight. Look at me! the position had shrieked.

People had looked. They had also come over to ask for more autographs and to congratulate the presenter on winning a recent 'Most Popular TV Personality' award. She had been gracious. With a smile here, a wriggle there and peals of girlish laughter, she had charmed everyone.

'You must've found the award extremely encouraging,' Kristin remarked.

'Not as encouraging as my contract to host the consumer services show.' An avaricious gleam lit the violet eyes. 'One point two million pounds!'

'It's a lot of money,' she said, for the contract, allied with Amanda's desire to promote her new show, was the reason for the interview.

'I shall make more, much, much more,' came the gleeful claim.

Kristin switched on her recorder. 'You started your career in local television,' she prompted.

'Yes, though I was soon asked to join a breakfast show which is shown nationwide.' There was a kittenish pout. 'You can't imagine how early I had to be at the studios.'

'Actually I can,' she said, smiling. 'Tomorrow morning I'm going on breakfast TV and the studio are sending a car at—'

'Just fancy,' her guest murmured, cutting in and cutting her off. 'My first newscast was—'

Amanda proceeded to detail her career history. This was followed by merry pronouncements about her 'interpersonal skills', 'feeling empowered' and how lucky she was to be so incredibly gifted. As she flitted on to buzz-word banalities about her plans for future projects, Kristin sighed. Several times she had tried to cut through the hype and reach something real, but without success.

'Would you like a pudding?' she enquired as their main-course plates were cleared away and dessert menus presented.

The choice of restaurant had made her wonder whether Amanda Cousins might be one of the 'gimme an expensive free lunch while I plug my show/record/film' species of celebrity, but it was not the case. While she had settled on Dover sole with garden-fresh vegetables, the presenter had ordered a green salad and proceeded to pick. It was clear that her idea of a meal was a lettuce leaf accompanied by a glass of fizzy water.

'No, thanks, I'll just take tea with lemon and no sugar,' Amanda replied. Drawing down the dark glasses, she fixed her gaze on the head waiter who hovered beside them, fluttered her lashes and sighed. 'I daren't annoy my personal fitness trainer by putting on too much weight.'

As if! Kristin thought as the head waiter launched into gushing reassurances. Her guest was fine-boned, fragile and as slim as a wand. In comparison, she felt like the chubby adolescent she once had been and awkwardly tall. And plain.

She studied the woman on the other side of the table. With her pansy eyes, heart-shaped face and swinging bob of lustrous brown hair, she was exquisite. It was no wonder that every female in the restaurant kept casting envious glances nor that the male customers were blatantly in thrall. As for the waiters, they had bowed and scraped to excess.

Yet behind the bubbly 'everyone's sweetheart' charm, she sensed a deliberate and even a cold person.

'Something from the sweet trolley, miss?' the head waiter enquired, speaking to her though he continued to send adoring glances in Amanda's direction.

'Sticky toffee pudding with clotted cream,' Kristin announced, in a spirit of what-the-hell defiance. 'And a cappuccino.'

Her guest's bill was going to be slight, so she might as well enjoy the cordon bleu cuisine, she rationalised. It would mean an extra session or two at the gym, but the food was a serious improvement on carry-out French fries.

'Everyone makes such a fuss of me,' Amanda said as the head waiter departed. Her delicate features took on a plaintive slant. 'Beauty can be such a great burden.'

'Poor duck,' Kristin could not resist saying, but her irony went unnoticed.

The woman might have beauty and brains—there could be no doubt she was a slick operator—but as modesty did not feature amongst her attributes, so she also lacked a sense of humour.

'Transport,' Amanda announced as Kristin finished the delicious pudding. 'I'd like you to pay my travelling expenses.'

'No problem,' she replied. 'If you tell me how much your taxis—'

'I'm not using taxis, I'm in a limousine.' A graceful hand casually swung. 'Three hundred pounds will cover it.'

She gaped. She knew that her guest lived in one of London's trendy city centre 'villages', which was a mere hop, skip and a jump away.

'Three hundred pounds?' she protested.

'I've hired a stretch Daimler for the day, from a friend who runs a local garage.' Amanda smiled. 'Maybe you noticed it parked outside?'

Kristin recalled an elegant silver car with a uniformed chauffeur seated at the wheel. 'Couldn't miss it,' she said.

'I'd like the money in cash,' came the brisk stipulation.

That morning she had withdrawn a generous sum from her expenses float so there were adequate notes in her purse, but should she object? She had scant idea of hire rates yet, for a deal done with a friend, three hundred pounds seemed suspiciously steep. In fact, it felt like extortion.

'Do you have a bill for the cost of the car?' she enquired.

'No.' Amanda pouted prettily. 'You're not going to kick

up a stink, are you?' she said, with a look which hinted that *she* could be winding up to throw a mean tantrum.

Kristin thought fast. A scene in the restaurant would be embarrassing enough, but, if thwarted, the presenter might decide to badmouth *The Ambassador* on her TV show.

'Good heavens, no,' she replied.

Stung! she thought as she handed over the money. The superwaif might have eaten almost nothing, yet she would be chauffeured around for the rest of the day at the newspaper's expense. And doubtless clutching some buckshee notes in her greedy little hand.

'Our readers will be interested in your personal life,' Kristin said, returning to the interview. 'Perhaps you'd care to say something about it?'

'I'm seeing Ralph Archibald at the moment. As you're probably aware, his father is an earl and owns vast estates. Ralphie adores me,' Amanda declared, and gave another gurgling laugh. 'I don't know why, but men seem to go silly over me. Matthew, your boss, was just the same.'

Kristin's jaw dropped. 'You—you used to go out with Matthew Lingard?' she faltered.

'This is off the record, but we had a heavy romance around—oh, ten years ago.'

Her mind flew back. The girl who had sat beside Matthew in the restaurant had had dark hair. Could it have been Amanda Cousins? The timing fitted and—now she remembered!—he had spoken of his girlfriend as Mandy. She frowned. He had also remarked on the incident ending their relationship.

'Matthew was devoted to me,' her companion continued, and shrugged slender shoulders. 'But...things happened and I felt compelled to tell him we were through. He was broken-hearted. I've seen him since at the occasional party, but he always avoids me. He hasn't recovered, you see. Perhaps he never will.'

Kristin crumpled up her white linen napkin. Matthew had told her to surprise him. He would be surprised to discover she had interviewed his ex-girlfriend—a breathtakingly beautiful girlfriend who, after listening to *her* accusations of sharp practice and female exploitation ten years ago, had decided to ditch him!

Matthew waited impatiently and, as the red light changed through amber to green, pushed his foot down hard on the accelerator. The Aston Martin sprang forward along the tree-lined avenue. At six o'clock in the morning, the London streets were quiet.

'How long do you reckon it'll take us?' asked Kristin, who was sitting beside him.

'Around thirty minutes and we have twenty, so we shouldn't be too adrift.'

'It's a good thing you rang the studios, otherwise we'd still both be waiting,' she said as they drove out towards the television centre which was on the western fringes of London. 'I don't understand how the woman could've been so specific on the times we were to be picked up and then forget to order the car.'

'Nor me, though I'm beginning to wish we weren't going on the damn programme.' Matthew shoved a hank of dark hair roughly back from his brow. 'I feel like death. I don't think I managed more than a couple of hours' sleep last night.'

'You were nervous about being interviewed?'

'No. When I've been on television before, it's always gone OK.'

'So what was the matter?'

'Just before I left the office yesterday evening, I heard that a couple of our competitors are planning cut-price promotions and intend to sell their papers at under half price.' His fingers tightened on the wheel, his knuckles draining white. 'That's what kept me awake.'

Kristin looked at him. 'But you must've known this might happen.'

'Sure. It's a cut-throat world and I expected one paper to go down that route, but not *two*.'

She saw the shadows beneath his eyes and the tenseness of his expression—and her heart went out to him.

'You're afraid our sales could be damaged?'

Matthew frowned out through the windscreen. He was not into baring his soul and admitting to doubts. He wasn't sure he should do so now, but he needed someone to talk to. A person whom he could trust. And, somehow, he knew he could trust her.

'Real men are allowed to worry,' Kristin said.

He gave a faint smile. 'I'm worried sick our sales might plummet. I've never admitted this to anyone before—apart from Sir George—but relaunching the paper is an extremely high-risk operation. It could turn out to be a dud.'

'Never,' she said. 'The other papers cutting their prices shows they're running scared and that's a good sign.'

'I guess,' he acknowledged.

'And they can't afford to cut their prices for long.'

'I'd say a month maximum, but—' Matthew broke off. The car had started to bump and was veering into the kerb. He straightened the swing and slowed. 'That's all we need,' he said, in a voice of exasperation. 'A puncture!'

Drawing to a halt, he cut the engine and clambered out of the car. Kristin got out, too.

'Is there anything I can do?' she asked as he scowled at the offside rear tyre which was decidedly flat and said something colourful.

He opened the boot, found a folded contraption of re-flective red plastic strips and handed it to her.

'You could stand this up behind us.'

He was surprised by her offer of help. He had, he real-ised, expected her to stand and impatiently watch while he laboured—and whinge about them being late. But she was not the whingeing kind.

As he took out a jack and became busy fixing it and raising the car, Kristin frowned. The contraption was a warning triangle which would alert other motorists to their stationary vehicle, but how did the thing slot together? She opened one side—and another. And closed them again.

'You don't want to get your jacket dirty, so shall I hold it?' she suggested.

Like her, Matthew had dressed smartly this morning and was wearing a pale grey suit with a chalk-blue shirt and darker blue Paisley-patterned tie.

'Thanks,' he said, peeling it off.

As he bent to unscrew wheel nuts, Kristin's gaze travelled across the width of his shoulders and down the length of his back. She could remember how smooth his skin had felt beneath her fingertips when they had been in bed at the castle. She watched him lift off the damaged wheel and fit on the spare. She could recall how muscular he had looked half-naked.

'You haven't managed it yet?' Matthew enquired, deftly replacing the wheel nuts.

'What? Oh.' She looked down at the triangle which she held in her hands and which she had forgotten. 'It's tricky.'

The wheel secured, he straightened. 'It's child's play,' he said, and with two swift movements he fixed the triangle into shape.

'Very clever,' she said.

'I'm brilliant,' he declared, and cocked a brow. 'Yes?'

Kristin heaved a noisy sigh. 'You're brilliant.'

'I knew you'd agree,' he said, grinning, and, leaning forward, he kissed the end of her nose.

It was a friendly, platonic, public kiss—yet it made her pulses race.

Why had he kissed her? Matthew wondered. Because she was pretty and funny and supportive—and so darned nice.

'Now perhaps you'd put the triangle down again,' Kristin said breathlessly.

'Will do. A request,' he said as he closed the boot. 'If you write in your column about the lame-brain who's unable to fix a simple warning sign, you don't make it me.'

'Spoilsport,' she said.

One thing she would not write in her column, she thought, was how she had looked at him and been bewitched by memories. And was bewitched now.

'Just protecting my reputation,' Matthew said, then looked at his hands and grimaced. They were streaked with black oil smears.

'Wait,' she instructed, when he started gingerly to extract a handkerchief from his trouser pocket.

Reaching for her bag, Kristin delved inside and found sachets containing dampened tissues, a legacy from a long-gone air journey. She tore open a couple of sachets and handed the tissues to him.

'Thanks,' he said, and wiped his hands.

Taking his jacket from her, he pulled it on and they climbed back into the car.

'The TV folk will've allowed a margin, so we should still be OK,' Matthew said as they resumed their journey. 'But pray there are no more hold-ups.'

'I'm praying. In a month's time the papers who cut their price will have lost money,' Kristin said, reverting to their earlier conversation, 'while *The Ambassador* will still be going and be even more into its swing. Which gives us an advantage.'

'True,' he conceded.

'You could drop it into the interview this morning that our competitors regard us as a threat and appear to be panicking, if not showing a tinge of desperation. You could say you regard it as a compliment.'

'And an admission that we're doing things right,' Matthew said thoughtfully. 'Then the people who haven't read the new-style *Ambassador* could be intrigued and decide to buy one.'

'And decide to stick with us.'

'For ever and ever,' he declared, and smiled. She had made him feel better, much better.

'Like you once said, you're taking a risk in employing

me,' Kristin said soberly. 'The success of the features could be an integral part of the paper's success and—' she chewed at her lip '—I hope I don't let you down.'

'Doubts?' he asked. 'But you've always seemed so sure.'

'I am. Mostly. However, I do lack newspaper experience and suppose—'

'You won't let me down.' Matthew grinned. 'I wouldn't allow it.'

She cast him an impatient look. 'Oh, don't be so—'

'Confident?'

Kristin laughed. 'Yes. What do I say if the breakfast-show interviewer should ask where I used to work?' she enquired, all of a sudden.

'You say *Trend*.'

'You don't mind?'

Matthew shook his head. 'The magazine is fresh and bright and innovative, and you've brought the same qualities to the newspaper.'

They were discussing the points which he wanted to be stressed on the programme, when the steel and smoked-glass bulk of the television complex appeared ahead.

'Made it,' he said.

'I shouldn't have worn this jacket,' Kristin declared, looking down at the black, red and white puppy-tooth jacket which she had teamed with a white top and a black skirt. 'It might zizz.'

'Zizz?'

'On the screen the check might—' she waggled her hand '—jitterbug. And my voice might croak and beads of sweat might gather on my top lip and my mind could go blank and—and the programme's live!' she wailed.

'I thought you had nerves of steel,' Matthew said.

'Of tissue paper. Oh, heavens, why did I ever agree to do this? I shall make a fool of myself and of the paper. I know it!'

'You want me to pull up and let you run screaming from the car?' he enquired.

'This minute.'

He put his hand on her knee. As she had calmed his fears and encouraged earlier, so he wanted to calm and encourage her now.

'You'll be fantastic,' he said.

Kristin gave a strained smile. His hand was warm and firm and reassuring. She was no longer fretting about her television debut, she was thinking about him…and her. Touching and entwined. In bed together.

'You're right. Well, perhaps not so much fantastic as passable,' she said, and he returned his hand to the wheel.

Five minutes later, they were being greeted by a production assistant and ushered into the hospitality room.

'We've restructured the show and you won't be appearing this morning,' the young man informed them.

Kristin stared. 'We aren't on?' she protested.

Thanks to her escort she had been psyched up and raring to go, and now she felt the downward swoop of anticlimax.

'Why not?' Matthew enquired.

'Last night an actress from one of the soaps appeared on a chat show and slammed the acting talents of her fellow performers. They demanded a chance to make an immediate rebuttal,' the young man explained, and nodded towards a television set in the corner of the room which showed a group of people talking and complaining all at the same time. 'It's such marvellous action that the director doesn't want to cut it off.'

'You let us get up at some unearthly hour and come all this way for nothing?' Matthew protested, a steely glitter in his blue eyes. 'Come under our own steam—stopping to change a tyre on the way—because you forgot to send a car.'

'Sorry about that, but you haven't come for nothing. Your interview will be recorded,' the production assistant informed him hastily, 'and shown as soon as possible.'

'I thought the programme went out live?'

There was a rueful smile. 'Sometimes we cheat a little.

But being recorded is to your benefit. Because we have more time, we'll be able to add some background stuff about the newspaper, go into greater depth and—'

'When do we do the interview?' he asked, breaking into the supposedly soothing spiel.

'In half an hour.'

Kristin stared at the computer screen. On her return from the riverside restaurant a couple of days ago, she had written up the interview with Amanda Cousins. Yesterday, when she had come back from the television studios, her words had been polished. The article had been pulled up again this afternoon, but she still wasn't happy. It seemed too bland, too flat. Too careful.

The problem was rooted in the fact that she had not liked the woman. The viewers might have voted her personality of the year and she might be fêted by a million adoring fans, but in her opinion she was a pain.

Kristin rested an elbow on the desk, her chin in her hand. It would be easy to do a demolition job and write acerbic remarks such as 'The last time I saw legs as thin, they were underneath a chicken', but trashing was not her style. Whilst other journalists did not hesitate to dip their pens in vitriol, she believed it was unfair to take cheap personal shots at someone and thus diminish their accomplishments.

Amanda Cousins was undoubtedly an accomplished presenter, but had she been as self-absorbed and mercenary when Matthew had known her? she wondered. Fame could change people so perhaps not, yet surely it did not rob them of a sense of humour?

Her brow creased. Did Matthew still hanker after his past love, as Amanda had stated? It had sounded more like ego-massaging to her. Yet when they had been together at Flytes Keep he had said he was dreaming about a beautiful dark-haired girlfriend. At the time she had not been sure whether she believed him, but now...

The presenter had provided sheets of publicity material,

plus a selection of photographs. Kristin took one out. Looking at the flawless face, she felt tempted to add a pair of spectacles. And a moustache. And a beard. And spots. Instead, she pressed the 'exit' key on her computer.

Matthew did not know about the lunch, so should she delete her article? But if she did she would be three hundred pounds out of pocket and when the interview failed to appear in the paper chances were Amanda Cousins would complain. There seemed little doubt that she kept a sharp eye on *all* her publicity.

'Conference time,' the financial editor called, and Kristin looked up to see that the various editors were making their way into Matthew's office.

Apart from her and the chief editorial writer who was a brisk, ultra-capable woman in her forties, all of them were men.

She followed, taking the last in a row of chairs which were curved around in front of his desk. At the morning conference it had been decided that the death of an elder statesman would lead on the front page, but a discussion quickly got underway as to whether a bribery scandal or the dramatic rescue of a potholer and his dog should take its place. The bribery idea lived for a while, but was dropped.

As the argument went back and forth, she looked at Matthew. He was sifting through papers, asking questions, making notes on a pad in a bold black scrawl. Kristin sat, fascinated by him and lost in the way he would write, then speak, stabbing his pen in the air for emphasis.

He had a habit, when he was thoughtful, of rubbing his thumb slowly across his lower lip. His lower lip was full. It was the lip of a Latin lover, she decided, while his thinner upper lip showed a more disciplined English reserve.

'What's your feel for it?' he asked, and she realised, with a start, that he was talking to her.

Kristin flushed, cleared her throat and tweaked at the

collar of the amber turtleneck which she wore with black trousers. She had stopped listening long ago.

'I'd go for the original story,' she rattled off, hoping she was talking sense. 'The man was loved and is a loss to the nation. We can run the pothole rescue second, with a big picture of the man's dog because people love dogs and—'

'You're with the general consensus,' Matthew said, stopping her mid-track. He nodded. 'That's how we'll play it.' He turned to the first page of his notes. 'Next thing—'

This time Kristin concentrated on what was being said.

'Will you hang on a moment?' he asked her as the meeting broke up and people pushed back their chairs and started to leave. He waited until everyone had dispersed, then closed his door. He turned to face her. 'I wanted to say that I appreciate all the hard work you and your team put into the cosmetic surgery article—you wrote it in double-quick time—and to tell you that it's had a good response.'

'It has?' she said delightedly.

He nodded. 'Several of the guys here have said how interesting they and their families found it, we've had calls from the public in praise, and I even had my sister on the phone lauding it to the skies. I think of Susan as Mrs Middle England, so if she likes it—' He grinned. 'You may just be a genius, Kristin.'

A wide smile spread across her face. Despite his comments about her fitting in and him not letting her fail, at the back of her mind had lurked the fear that after three months he would say she was not quite good enough. Now that fear faded.

'I aim to please,' she said.

She wondered whether she should tell him she had had lunch with Amanda Cousins—and warn him that she would be submitting a mammoth expense chit—but was reluctant to spoil the moment.

'Do you have any more brainwaves?' Matthew enquired as she got to her feet.

'How about a series of articles about working mothers?' she suggested. 'We could interview women who'd found it difficult to combine a job with a family and others who manage and believe it benefits their kids. If the women covered a wide range—'

He shook his head. 'It's an old argument.'

'But not a tired one,' Kristin said, and walked towards him. 'Work versus motherhood is a nice tight emotional issue, an issue with legs, and if we present it in a different way—'

She broke off to look down. When the editorial group had pulled back their chairs, one of the rugs had become rumpled. It was also torn and, somehow, she had caught her ankle-booted foot in the hole. She kicked out, attempting to free herself, and stumbled.

'Careful!' Matthew warned.

He stepped forward and as his arms circled around her she fell against him.

'Thanks,' she said.

She *did* please, he thought. She was doing a fine job as features editor, she had shown an easy manner in yesterday's TV interview and—he liked holding her.

'You're not safe to be let out alone,' he rebuked her, with a grin. 'One minute you're falling into a puddle, the next you're tumbling headlong over a rug. It's a good job you have me around to save you.'

'You sat me in the puddle,' Kristin protested breathlessly.

He was holding her close. Close enough for her to be aware of his lean male strength. Close enough for her to feel as if she could drown in the blue of his eyes. So close that the air was filled with a throbbing sexuality.

All of a sudden, Matthew became aware of a stillness in the general office outside. Lifting his gaze, he looked out through the glass.

'We've been spotted,' he said.

As she followed his gaze, her cheeks flushed pink.

Everyone from the office boy to the deputy editor was watching them.

'Oh, heavens,' she said, in dismay.

'I guess we'd better face the music and…perform.'

'Which means?'

'This,' he said, and his mouth covered hers in a kiss which started off soft and tender, but ended up disturbingly passionate.

Applause rang out from all around the general office. There were cheers and whistles and shouts of 'Cor blimey!' When he drew away and Kristin looked beyond him, she saw that every person was on their feet, clapping and smiling broadly. The colour in her cheeks deepened from pink to scarlet.

'I thought we were supposed to have a working relationship, pure and simple,' she said, a little shakily.

Matthew grinned. 'So did I, but—' He moved his shoulders. 'Maybe we should announce our engagement. A pretend engagement. People seem to be forever wanting to know when I'm going to find myself a bride and that'd get them off my back. How about it?'

She stared at him. 'You're crazy.'

'Then how about taking a bow?' he said, and took hold of her hand.

Together, they bowed to their audience. The applause grew louder. There were more whistles and cheers.

'Encore!' someone called, but Matthew shook his head.

He opened his door. 'Back to work,' he instructed, in a businesslike tone, and Kristin sped back to her desk.

He had gone crazy, Matthew thought as he sat down. There had been an element of playing to his audience, but he had wanted to kiss her. He had needed to kiss her. Again. Yet by kissing her so publicly—and with such devotion—he had given the office grapevine plenty reason to gossip.

As for his talk of announcing their engagement, what

dumbfool thought process had come up with that suggestion? he wondered. And why?

Once again, Kristin put the Amanda Cousins article up on her computer screen. She changed a word here, and another one there, and tried to look as if she was concentrating. On the surface, the office appeared to have returned to normality, but she was aware that all around her people must be wondering about her relationship with Matthew. And were no doubt speculating on whether or not she was sleeping with the boss.

She had decided that the article was complete and she would print it out to read again, when she saw Emily making her way down the office.

'What're you doing here?' she asked after they'd exchanged greetings.

'It's a school holiday and Daddy and I are going to a concert, so we decided I'd join him here. How are you getting along?' The girl looked back to where Matthew was sitting at his desk, his dark head bowed. 'Is it working out with the delicious Mr Lingard?'

'It's working out well,' Kristin said, grateful that her visitor had not arrived a few minutes earlier. '*The Ambassador* is doing well, too.'

'I know. Daddy's delighted.' Emily lowered her voice into a conspiratorial whisper. 'This is a secret so don't tell anyone, but he's thinking of inviting all the editors to our villa in Italy for a ''thank you'' weekend. He's done it before, with directors of his other companies.'

'Sounds like fun.'

'It will be. The villa is in Portofino. Have you been there?'

She shook her head. 'I've never been to Italy.'

'Portofino is a lovely little port, with pavement cafés overlooking the water. The villa isn't big enough for Daddy to invite everyone at the same time, like he did at Flytes

Keep,' the girl continued, 'so the invitations'll need to be staggered.'

'Will you be there?'

Emily turned down her mouth. 'No, I have exams this summer, so I have to stay at home and study. Then I'm due to visit an old spinster aunt. Working mothers,' she said, suddenly picking up a list of ideas which Kristin had jotted down and reading from it. 'Will you be writing about them?'

'No.'

'Why not?'

'Matthew isn't keen. I suggested it to him, but—' Kristin shrugged. 'I'll come up with something else which he will agree with.'

'Daddy was telling me that the two of you were interviewed for breakfast TV. How did it go?'

'To begin with I was petrified, but Matthew helped me along and—' she grinned '—the director reckoned we did a great job in promoting the paper and that we're both television naturals.'

'Do you know when the interview's likely to be shown?'

She shook her head. 'It could be any time soon. I set my video to record the programme this morning, but apparently our bit wasn't on.'

'Sorry to intrude, but can I have a word?' asked Pete, an industrious, rather worthy young man who worked on her team. 'It's about—'

'I'm off,' Emily said quickly. 'It's been good to see you again.'

'And you. Let me know the next time you're coming to Hammersmith and perhaps we can sneak out together and grab a coffee.'

The teenager grinned. 'I'd like that. Bye.'

'Goodbye,' Kristin said, and turned to speak to the reporter.

The matter discussed and settled, she printed out the Amanda Cousins interview and read it through. She rose to her feet. She had shilly-shallied long enough. Matthew was alone in his office and she would show the piece to him.

'Please would you look at this?' she requested, handing it over.

He started to read, then his head shot up. 'You interviewed Amanda Cousins?' he said, his expression abruptly tense.

'Earlier in the week. Her agent was keen, and she's just won an award and been given a lucrative contract. Amanda is well-known and much loved—'

'She is,' Matthew said brusquely.

'And I thought our readership would be interested in her.'

'For sure,' he muttered, and read the article. As he reached the end, he frowned. 'I used to know Amanda,' he began slowly.

Kristin nodded. 'She said.'

His face took on a guarded look. 'What did she say?'

'Just that the two of you had had a romance, but it was a long time ago.' She paused. 'Amanda is beautiful.'

'Perfection,' he rasped.

'I ought to warn you that my expenses for the lunch are going to be hefty,' she continued. 'Amanda had hired a limousine—'

'Don't worry about it.'

'But it cost three hundred pounds. Cost the paper three hundred pounds.'

'That's OK,' Matthew said, and passed the article back to her over his desk. 'Sounds fine.'

As she walked out of his office, Kristin was pensive. She had decided that Amanda's comment about Matthew not recovering from their relationship should be taken with a sizeable pinch of salt. He might have said he would never forget his girlfriend, but the romance was ten years ago. Yet his unquestioning acceptance of the woman hiring a costly car seemed evidence of a soft spot and his tension indicated that he could still be pining for her.

Was that why he had suggested they embark on a pretend engagement which would stop people pushing him to get married? she wondered. Had Matthew decided that if he could not have Amanda Cousins for his bride he would remain single—for ever?

CHAPTER SEVEN

IT WAS eight-thirty on Saturday evening. Beth had gone off earlier, dressed to kill, to meet up with friends for a merry night out; all over the capital the bars, clubs and discos would be swinging, but Kristin was standing on the top of a small set of steps cleaning her bedroom windows. She had no grumbles.

After devoting most of Friday to writing her *Trend* column, she had planned to spend her second day off catching up on domestic matters, but she had slept in late. This meant she had luxuriated over her breakfast for a full five minutes before rushing off to keep her time slot at the gym. There she had dutifully biked and rowed and treadmilled, then galloped back to the flat to change.

It was her turn to do the weekend shopping, so she had sped out again to the neighbourhood supermarket. Coming back, she had thrust a pile of bedlinen and dirty clothes into the washing machine, eaten a late lunch, then located duster and polish, damp cloth et cetera. It was also her turn to clean the first-floor flat. The two bedrooms had been industriously tidied and vacuumed, plus the cream-walled, cream-carpeted living room and finally the flight of stairs which led down to the private front door.

As she had started on the ironing, and Beth had departed, the phone had rung. Her mother had called for a chat. It had been a long chat. When the ironing had been belatedly completed, she had microwaved a cheese-filled jacket potato and, with the sun beginning to sink in a pink-gold sky, had decided to wash the windows.

Climbing down, Kristin dropped the chamois leather into the bucket. She had had the chance to go out this evening, she thought, and wrinkled her nose. When she had been at the supermarket, she had rounded a pyramid of baked bean tins and come face to face with James, who lived a few doors away. Tall, fair and in his late twenties, James did something financial in the City.

When he had moved into the road a few months ago the young man had had a girlfriend—though that had not stopped him from showing a decided interest in *her*—but the girlfriend had been discarded. Now James was eager for them to become a pair. He had been suggesting a date tonight when an elderly shopper had blundered between them and straight into the baked beans. As tins had started to cascade, she had made a hasty claim of 'Sorry, I'm busy' and escaped.

Whilst she liked her neighbour, she had no wish to become involved. He was pleasant and personable, but, for her, he lacked the X factor—that indefinable something which inspired attraction. He was not a man with whom she felt any urge to tangle—as she did with Matthew. She enjoyed tangling with him—verbally, professionally…and sexually.

Snapping shut the steps, Kristin hauled them and the bucket back across the living room and into the kitchen. She had also planned to have a day switched off from thoughts of the office and thoughts of her boss, yet he had kept popping into her mind. If she went out with James, maybe it would stop her thinking about him so much. Emptying the bucket, she refilled it with clean warm water. Or maybe it wouldn't.

She positioned the steps beside the sink. The house was old with high ceilings and sash windows and, hemmed in by the sink and side cupboards, the kitchen window was difficult to reach. Heeling off her canvas shoes, she climbed up to stand barefoot on the draining board. She was precariously balancing when the doorbell rang.

Kristin sighed. Could this be James? Had he recognised her supermarket words as evasion, spotted her in the bedroom a few minutes earlier and arrived to invite her out again? She clambered back to floor level. If so, she would tell him it was too late.

Tugging at the droopy-necked caramel-coloured top which she wore with frayed denim shorts—her house-cleaning get-up—she padded barefoot down the stairs. She would also find some way of saying, gently but firmly, that she was not interested in him.

But when she opened the front door her pulses jolted. On the path stood a tall, dark-haired, broad-shouldered figure, silhouetted against the golden glow of the evening light.

'Oh,' she said, in surprise. 'I thought you were James.'

'Who's James?' Matthew enquired.

'A guy who lives along the road. We're—um—friendly,' she said, and raised a hand to shade her eyes. Now she could see him better, and now she saw that he was tight-lipped and frowning. 'Is something wrong?'

'You bet it is,' he replied. 'You thought I wouldn't recognise you?'

'Excuse me?'

'You imagined that when you provided the photograph I wouldn't remember?'

'Which photograph?' Kristin asked, and was suddenly aware of her old clothes and untidy appearance. She attempted to smooth down her tousled lion's mane of tawny hair. 'Provide it to whom?'

'Don't play the innocent,' he said.

'I'm not playing anything,' she protested. 'I have no idea what you're talking about.'

'The breakfast show interview,' he said tersely. 'It was aired this morning.'

'I haven't seen it.'

Matthew scowled. For the first time since the relaunch of the newspaper, today he had stayed away from the office. He had enjoyed a long lie-in and arisen refreshed and re-invigorated. After a quick trip onto the High Street to restock his fridge, he had gone for a run in Hyde Park. Later, he had swum. He had felt relaxed, until this evening when he had played the video recording.

Then he had climbed furiously into his car and driven straight over, but he had assumed she would have watched the interview, too. He had also assumed Kristin would be wearing the kind of clothes she wore at the office, not be decked out in a baggy top and shorts, and looking appealingly tumbled with her hair loose around her shoulders.

'If you had—' he began, then broke off. 'Are you alone?'

'I am. Would you like to come in?'

He gave a brusque nod. The warm evening meant there were people strolling along the street, and he had no wish to quarrel with her in public.

'Please.'

Kristin gestured for him to enter the hallway, then closed the door and set off back up the stairs. He followed. Her denim shorts were short and, Matthew thought irritably, the view he had of her legs and backside must be sending his blood pressure soaring.

'So what's this about a photograph?' she asked as they went into the living room which overlooked the leafy green of the back garden.

'Somebody supplied one of you to the breakfast show people.'

'Not guilty.'

He frowned. 'Then how did they get hold of it?'

'I've no idea, but what did they want a picture of me for?' Kristin enquired.

'You remember the production assistant spoke of them putting in background about the newspaper? They did a potted history of *The Ambassador*, but they also added some extra info about me and you. They described my career and referred to your time with *Trend*, plus they showed a shot of you as a model.'

Her blood ran cold. 'Oh, heavens,' she said, her voice suddenly fraught. 'Not when I was—'

'Bare-breasted?' Matthew rasped. 'No. You were fully clothed.'

She sagged with relief. To have been displayed semi-nude on television was the stuff of which nightmares were made.

'Thank goodness.'

'Fully clothed, with short cropped hair and skinny, and—' his eyes burned into hers '—recognisable as the girl who marched into a restaurant all those years ago and poured a jug of water over my head!'

'You deserved it,' she said.

'Like hell! Ka, you called yourself then, but now it's Kristin.' His lip twisted. 'I wonder why?'

His anger was mixed with hurt. He liked her—had even been growing fond—and had believed he could trust her, so to discover that she had been deceiving him *wounded*.

'I was called Ka by the model agency and only the agency, because there was another Kristin on their books,' she said. 'I've never used the name myself.'

'You didn't put modelling on your c.v.,' Matthew accused.

'That was because it didn't seem relevant and because it happened at a difficult time in my life. A time which I'd rather forget.' She frowned. 'I wasn't trying to trick you. I just...didn't remind you.'

'Same difference. If I hadn't seen the photograph on TV, I would never've made the connection. But when Sir George approached you about working for *The Ambassador* you—' he pointed a condemning finger '—knew who I was.'

Kristin shook her head. 'No.'

'Back in the past, you'd tracked me down to the restaurant,' he said impatiently, 'so—'

'All I knew was that you were the deputy editor of the colour supplement and responsible for the shots being printed. No one told me your name and I didn't ask. I was too wound up. When we first met at Flytes Keep, I thought

I'd seen you before and I soon remembered where. But I was keen to land the features editor job, so—' she moved her shoulders '—I kept quiet.'

'Ambition ruled supreme,' Matthew jibed. 'And you've been keeping quiet ever since.'

'I couldn't see the point in resurrecting the episode and disrupting things,' she said defensively.

'You disrupted everything ten years ago, in spades! Though, of course, the clever bit was crying.'

Kristin frowned. 'What do you mean?'

'If you'd stuck to hurling abuse and throwing the water, the guy I was dining with would've sympathised with me. Laughed himself silly, no doubt,' he said sardonically, 'but been sympathetic. However—'

'Who was the man?' she cut in. 'Who was your would-be employer?'

'Thomas Kinnear.'

'Oh, crikey,' she said.

Thomas Kinnear ran a media empire of newspapers and periodicals, television and radio stations which stretched from the States to Europe to South-East Asia. A softly spoken American who kept a low personal profile, he wielded immense power in the world of big-league journalism.

'Quite,' Matthew said coldly, and continued, 'However, your tears persuaded him that I really was callous, willing to exploit and not someone whom he wanted on his payroll. Yes, crying was a real cute ploy.'

'It wasn't a ploy.'

'Come on,' he derided. 'I can understand that you mightn't have been too thrilled to discover shots of yourself semi-nude in a national newspaper, but you're not the kind of girl who'd weep over it.'

'I'm not now,' Kristin said, 'but I was then.'

His eyes narrowed. 'Your tears were genuine? You weren't acting the drama queen?'

'No. Why should I?'

'Because women do—to try and achieve their aims. Some women.'

'Not this one. Would you like a drink?' she asked, when he frowned and fell silent.

Matthew hesitated. He had not come to socialise, but his throat was dry and the suggestion appealed. 'Do you have a beer?'

'Two kinds. Come and choose,' she said, and led him through to the narrow kitchen with its walls of white units. She showed him the cans which were lined up in the fridge door. 'Help yourself.'

'Thanks. Don't bother with a glass,' he said, ripping the ring-pull tab off a can of chilled lager and taking a swig. 'You're not having one?'

'Not yet. I was cleaning the windows and—' Kristin looked at the steps and bucket '—if you don't mind I'd like to finish before the light goes.'

'Carry on,' he said.

As she climbed onto the draining board and began to wield the leather, Matthew turned to look back through to the living room. With a rose-patterned sofa and armchairs, pine bookshelves and round coffee table which carried a vase of mimosa and pink carnations, the room was attractive. It was also neat and tidy; every surface shone.

'You seem to have been busy,' he remarked.

Kristin smiled. 'Today I've had a blitz.'

'Do you like housework?'

'Don't tell anybody, but I do. I find it good for the soul.' Standing on tiptoe, she reached into the top corner of the window. 'Those photographs truly upset me,' she said.

'But you paraded up and down catwalks,' Matthew protested, still dubious about her claim of real tears, 'and you were all of—what, eighteen?'

She bobbed her head. 'I was a young and sheltered eighteen,' she said, climbing down, 'and, whilst I managed to look the confident model, I was actually painfully shy. And naive.'

'Let me,' he said, when she folded the steps and made to move them. 'Where do you want to be?'

'The living room, please,' Kristin said, and directed him towards the first of two tall sash windows, the top halves of which refused to open, due to the repeated application of coats of paint. 'Thanks. My first reaction when my father showed me the photographs—'

'Your father discovered them?' he interrupted.

'Yes, Dad prides himself on being well-informed and buys all the quality Sunday papers. My first reaction was disbelief. I hadn't realised the shots had been taken,' Kristin said, and as she cleaned the lower half of the window she explained.

'What was your father's response?' he enquired.

She winced, remembering. 'Outrage and disgust.'

'Why disgust?' He leant a broad shoulder against the wall. 'OK, you were naked from the waist up, but they weren't prurient pictures.'

'I told him that, but he declared that only a fine line separated them from spreads in girlie magazines.' She turned. 'He also insisted that I'd posed on purpose and—and he made me feel like a slut.'

'Hey,' Matthew said. She had broken off to swallow and look at him with eyes which were suspiciously bright. Straightening, he stretched out a hand to touch her arm. 'You're not getting weepy on me?'

'And risk shattering my street cred? No way,' she declared resolutely, and climbed the steps to begin wiping the upper window. 'I tried to convince myself that other people were unlikely to notice the photos and if they did they'd simply shrug. However, we lived on site at the school where my father worked and when I walked through the grounds the next day there were groups of boys watching me.'

'The colour supplement had gone the rounds?'

'Yes. The younger boys sniggered and there was surreptitious lip-licking and obscene gestures from the older ones. It went on for weeks.'

Matthew frowned. Her back was to him so he could not see her face, but he could hear the emotion and remembered pain in her voice.

'Nasty,' he said.

'I felt so humiliated and so *cheapened*. Some of the stricter parents rang to state their disapproval, which had my father apoplectic and earned me another roasting. Then the tabloid reporter turned up—'

'The tabloids took an interest?' he asked, in surprise.

'One of the sleaziest,' Kristin said, and quoted the name. She looked down at him. 'I thought it was you who had given them my address.'

'I didn't know it. All I knew was that you were a model called Ka. But I would never've put a tabloid on to you. Least of all that one.'

'Well, somehow their reporter found out where I lived, knocked on the door and asked if I'd pose for topless nudie shots.'

'And your father hit the roof again?'

'No. He sent the reporter away and then said, very quietly and sadly, how disappointed he was in me.'

Matthew frowned. 'Which must've been worse than him being angry,' he observed.

'It almost crucified me.'

Kristin was silent for a moment, then she rallied and explained how she had gone to the photographer's studio, on to the newspaper, and finally landed up at the restaurant.

She gave a rueful smile. 'I rushed in and you know the rest.'

'Does your father still insist that you knowingly posed for the shots?' he enquired.

'No, eventually he recognised that I'd simply been... gauche. Though it took a while.'

As she turned to complete her window-cleaning, Matthew took a drink of his lager. She was stretching up and the curves of her backside were just visible beneath the denim of her shorts. Her top had slipped sideways to reveal a smooth shoulder. He swallowed another mouthful. His libido was being aggressively tweaked.

'When you first attacked me I wondered if it was a publicity stunt,' he said. 'Although you seemed to be alone, I half expected flashbulbs to pop and had visions of seeing myself in the papers the next day—soaking wet and looking like an idiot.'

'Then I'd sell my side of the story to the highest bidder and use the episode as a springboard to fame?'

'Careers have been built on less.'

Turning, Kristin shook her head. 'I was as surprised as you were when I doused you with the water, but it was your own fault,' she said earnestly. 'You were the one who'd selected and printed the shots, so you were the person whom I needed to punish. As I'd been punished.'

'I didn't select the bare-breasted shots,' Matthew said.

Confusion rippled her brow. 'But I was told—'

'Although I saw them, I'd chosen three or four perfectly respectable photos to accompany the article, but one of my assistants changed them over at the last minute without my knowledge.'

She gazed down at him. 'So you weren't responsible?'

'Not personally, though it was my ultimate responsibility. The guy did it for a joke. To spice things up, or so he said later. I ought to have spotted the switch, but—' he frowned '—at the time I had other things on my mind and I didn't.'

'When did you realise what'd happened?'

'When the editor summoned me into his office and shoved a copy of the supplement under my nose. He informed me that this was not the kind of image which we wanted to project and I was severely reprimanded.' Tipping back his head, Matthew drained the can. 'The irony was that the circulation figures rose for that issue and for the next couple of weeks—in expectation of more of the same. Like your editor at *Trend* remarked, sex sells.'

'I was far too impetuous,' Kristin said, chastising herself. 'I ought to have checked my facts.'

He gave a wry smile. 'It would've saved me a wetting.'

'I'm sorry.'

'I'm sorry the shots caused you so much upset,' Matthew responded.

'A couple of people at *Trend* know I used to model,' she said suddenly, 'so they could've told the breakfast show people and helped track down a photograph. And,' she went on, 'perhaps it was your assistant who found out my address and gave it to the tabloid reporter all those years ago—for another joke?'

He shook his head. 'The guy was reprimanded, too, by the editor and by me, and he was so subdued afterwards he would never've risked it. But that particular tabloid has its own devious sources.' He pointed to the top of the window. 'You've missed a bit.'

'I can't reach it.'

'If you come down, I'll do it.'

'Thanks,' she said.

Matthew rinsed out the leather, twisted it in his fists to wring out the surplus water, then climbed onto the flat top of the steps. As he stretched, sweeping a long arm back and forth across the window, his short-sleeved navy shirt tugged free from his jeans and rode up to reveal a strip of olive-skinned back.

Kristin's fingertips started to tingle. Once more, she thought of how she had stroked his back and felt the texture of his skin when they had been in bed.

'If you were so shy, how come you decided to go into modelling?' he enquired.

She jerked out of her reverie. 'Excuse me?'

'You said you were a shy eighteen, so—'

'It was by chance, not from choice,' Kristin said hastily, and explained how the agent had spotted her. 'When I told my parents, my mother suggested I take a gap year before university and model, because it'd be lucrative and the chance probably wouldn't come again, but my father was dead against the idea.'

'Is that OK?' Matthew asked, indicating his handiwork.

'Perfect.'

'Shall I do the other top one?'

She grinned, thinking that he seemed equally at home cleaning windows as he did running a newspaper.

'Please.'

He came down, moved the steps and climbed aboard again. The dampened leather was put to work.

'What did you feel about the suggestion that you model?' he queried.

'I wasn't interested in modelling as such, but it offered a chance to rebel. So I declared that I wasn't going to university *ever* and enrolled with the agency the very next day.'

'Why the need to rebel?'

'My parents had been divorced a short time earlier and I wanted to make them pay for messing up my life and make them suffer.' Kristin exhaled a breath. 'Though, in fact, it was me who paid by missing out on college.'

'You once mentioned going haywire when you were young; this was you rebelling against the divorce?'

'Yes. My parents thought I was old enough to take it in my stride, but—' She paused. Although it had happened a long time ago, whenever she thought about the break-up an ache formed in the pit of her stomach. 'I didn't find it easy to be philosophical.'

The window cleaned, Matthew climbed down. 'Do you want to talk about it?'

She considered his suggestion. Although she had written about certain aspects of the upheaval, she had rarely spoken about it—but his blue eyes were warm and, all of a sudden, she wanted to speak to him.

'Please,' she said. 'Would you like another lager?'

He nodded. 'Window-cleaning is thirsty work.'

Kristin collected a second beer and a can of cola for herself from the fridge. When she returned, Matthew was sitting on the couch and, after handing him his drink, she sat down at the other end.

'Perhaps it was because I was an only child, or because, living in the school grounds in a contained society, I was cocooned—I don't know,' she began. 'But when it dawned on me that my parents weren't happy together it seemed as if my world had come to an end.'

'Which your childhood world had,' he said.

'Yes.'

'When did you realise your folks weren't happy?'

'Just a few months before they split up.' Kristin swallowed a taste of cola. 'I think I'd known something was wrong for a couple of years, but I ignored it in the hope it'd go away.'

'Understandable,' Matthew said, and reached out to stroke the back of her hand gently. 'And you feeling upset now is understandable, too.'

She smiled. 'Thanks. By the time my parents separated, I'd got myself in a mess emotionally,' she went on, 'and—although I was shy, I'd always been wilful and a little spoilt—and for a while I became the teenager from hell.'

'It was sex, drugs and rock 'n' roll?'

'I had the sense to keep clear of reckless sex and drugs, but I went through a procession of boyfriends, one of whom played in a heavy metal band. But all of them either wore earrings or had weird haircuts or sported tattoos. My father used to throw a fit when he saw them.'

'Which was the whole idea.'

Kristin shone a wry grin. 'Of course. I thought I'd had a hard deal,' she said, her grin fading, 'but I suspect that no matter how old you are when it happens—twenty, thirty, forty even—if your parents get divorced it leaves a scar on your heart.'

'Probably,' he agreed, thinking how fortunate he was to have happy and devoted parents.

'And there's always a child in your head who wants Mummy and Daddy to get together again,' she said, and he heard a pang of wistfulness in her voice.

'You once spoke of your mother walking out,' Matthew said. 'Did she institute the divorce?'

Kristin nodded. 'Mum was only twenty when they married. She says that for a long time she was willing to trot obediently along beside my father, doing whatever he wanted, but as she approached her forties she began to feel trapped. She longed to go to new places and do things on the spur of the moment. Catch up on the madness of youth, if you like.'

'Which she'd missed by marrying at twenty.'

'Right. However, Dad prefers a structured life and is big on respectability.'

'He feels that, as a headmaster, he should set a good example?' he enquired.

'Yes. When he was given his present appointment, he'd reached his goal and was content, but my mother looked at the future and saw boredom.'

'Then she met a guy who wasn't boring?'

'You guessed.'

'I've been around long enough to know these things,' Matthew said drily. 'And the guy was—?'

'Rex, who became my stepfather. He calls himself an artisan blacksmith. He makes iron gates and fireguards and odd metal sculptures. He only works when the mood takes him, wanders around in old clothes—'

'Not jeans?' he asked, in mock protest.

Kristin grinned. 'I'm afraid so. And he wears torn shirts.'

He looked down. 'My shirt isn't torn.'

'No, but it has a button missing.'

'Where?'

She reached out. 'There,' she said, and found her fingers sliding beneath the navy cotton to touch firm warm flesh.

'Are you making a pass at me?' Matthew enquired.

She sat back. 'You think I'd be so obvious?'

'You might.'

'And I might not. Rex doesn't give a damn about what anyone else thinks of him,' Kristin continued. 'I find him a bit too laid-back and cavalier, but my mother fell for him.'

'Because he was so different to your father.'

'I'm sure that's a part of the attraction,' she agreed. 'Dad keeps a pretty tight lid on his emotions, whereas Rex lets it all hang out. Anyhow, my mother departed while I stayed with my father and I started to lose weight.'

'You became anorexic?'

'No, but I felt so stressed that I found it difficult to eat. I'd been at what my mother called "the puppy fat stage", but suddenly the pounds began to drop off. I became all cheek and hip bones, which is why the model agent noticed me.'

Matthew cocked a brow. 'But you still had a bosom.'

'Enough.'

'Though you're more luxuriously endowed now,' he said, and his gaze fleetingly dipped. 'How long did you model?'

'For seven or eight months,' Kristin replied, wanting to cross her arms over her chest. At his look, her pulse rate had quickened and she had felt her nipples start to tighten. But becoming aroused just by a mere look was pathetic. 'After I'd soaked you, I dashed straight to the agency and told them I was quitting.'

'Which must've helped mend things with your father.'

'It did, though then he wanted me to try for a university place and I wouldn't.'

'You were still making him suffer?'

She nodded. 'I'd earned an astonishing amount of money from modelling,' she continued, 'so I bought myself this flat and enrolled at secretarial college. Dad believed my leaving home was yet another rebellion, but I needed to get away, stop seeing myself as a victim and grow up. Which I did.'

'Was your father pleased when you got on so well at *Trend*?' Matthew enquired.

'No. Like you did, he mocked the magazine and me.'

His brow furrowed. 'I shouldn't have mocked.'

'Too right,' Kristin said, and dug him in the ribs.

'That hurt!' he protested, rearing back.

'It was meant to.'

'But your father must be proud of you now?'

'He's delighted I'm on the staff of a broadsheet like *The Ambassador*—he feels that, at long last, I'm using my brains—but I'd need to interview someone like a world-famous academic or a head of state before he'd be truly proud.' She cast him a look. 'I'm sorry I ruined your chance to work for Thomas Kinnear.'

'I was sorry, too, for a long time, though much of my anger was tied up with the fact that I thought you were pulling a stunt,' Matthew said, and smiled. 'But it's turned out fine. Kinnear would never've allowed me to become the editor of one of the papers which he owns at my current tender age.'

'You don't think so?'

'I'm sure.'

'Which means,' Kristin said, grinning, 'that in prompting him to withdraw his job offer, which forced your career onto a path which eventually led to taking charge of *The Ambassador*, I did you a favour.'

'I guess. Though it doesn't mean you can chuck jugs of water over me in future.'

'You have no sense of adventure,' she complained.

'Like hell I don't,' Matthew retorted, and he kissed her.

His mouth was warm and firm. As his tongue probed, parting her lips, she tasted the faint flavour of lager—and tasted him. It was a heady mixture which made her senses whirl.

'Adventurous or not?' he demanded, pulling back.

She gazed at him. 'Well—'

'You need more proof,' he declared, and he kissed her again.

This time his mouth lingered on hers. There was a dreamy twining of tongues and a flickering need which had her moving closer. As her arms slid up around his neck, the kiss deepened. The need grew.

Easing away, he skimmed kisses down over the line of her jaw to the silken column of her throat. He pushed aside the neck of her loose cotton top and pressed his lips to her naked shoulder. Her flesh felt cool beneath his hot mouth. For a long delicious moment, he indulged in the taste of her skin and her subtle fragrance, then his hand pushed beneath the caramel cotton.

He felt the smoothness of her midriff and the material of her bra. He cupped the fullness of her breasts enclosed in white satin, but then, needing more, he reached around her back to unfasten hooks.

'Naked,' he muttered, and as his hands covered her breasts he drew in a controlling breath.

She was all smooth skin and luscious curves. They were curves which he needed to gaze upon, curves which he had to taste. He peeled the loose top off over her head and tossed aside her bra. As he looked down at her honeyed breasts with their tight rose-brown nipples, his body hardened into aching desire and he felt his heart start to pump.

He rubbed his thumbs across the pointed tips and Kristin arched her spine. His touch was impassioned, not gentle, but she did not want gentle. She wanted to feel, to writhe, to reach the heavens. He touched her again, dragging her nipples from side to side in a way which had her biting into her lip and arching closer.

'Matt,' she breathed, and tugged desperately at his shirt. She needed to touch him.

'Careful; I don't want to lose any more buttons,' he warned, smiling against her mouth.

Unfastening his shirt, she slid it from his shoulders and

gazed at the smooth olive torso which was overlaid with a black lace of hair. She caressed him, fingering the flat brown discs of his nipples, then leaned closer. Kristin dragged her breasts across his chest and felt the erotic rasp of hair against the sensitive tips. Her breathing quickened—and so did his.

Lowering her back against the soft cushions, Matthew bent his head and kissed her breasts. He tongued them. Dimly he remembered how, when they had first met, he had felt she was designed for passion and the movement of her body against his told him that when they made love she would be wonderfully uninhibited and excitingly wanton.

He sucked on her breasts and felt her fists tighten in the hair on the top of his head. His desire built. He had wanted her for so long, fantasised so often about how it would have been at the castle if the damned alarm clock had not rung, and now...

'I'm too old for this,' he murmured.

Kristin eased back to focus on him. 'Too old for—for what?' she asked jerkily.

'Snogging on the sofa.'

'You call this snogging?' she said, her hazel eyes shining.

'No, I call it foreplay.' He drew in a draught of air. 'But I can't make love to you here. I need to make love to you in bed. Only—'

'Only what?' she enquired, when he frowned.

'I didn't expect...this and I haven't come...prepared.'

'That's OK. I'm on the pill.'

Matthew smiled. 'Such an efficient girl,' he said and, rising to his feet, he pulled her up beside him. 'Which is your room?'

Kristin pointed to a door which stood half open. 'That one.'

'Let's go,' he said, his arm around her waist, then he stopped and listened.

There was the sound of a key turning in a lock and, a
moment later, a female voice shouted up from downstairs.

'Kris, I'm home. I know it's early, but I've brought some
of the gang back with me for a drink. They're just parking
their cars.'

They looked at each other.

'It's Beth, my flatmate,' she told him.

Matthew swore. He wanted her so desperately and to be
thwarted now, a second time, was almost more than he
could bear. It set his teeth on edge. It made him want to
howl with loss and anger. But they could not be intimate—
could not explore and enjoy that intimacy—if there were
people sitting in the next room.

He bent to retrieve his shirt from the floor. 'Get dressed,'
he said, doing up the buttons. 'We can't. Not now.'

'No,' Kristin agreed, and swiftly pulled on her bra and
top.

A minute or two later, footsteps sounded on the stairs
and a cheerful curly-haired brunette appeared in the doorway.

'Oh—hello,' she said. She looked interestedly at
Matthew, then smiled at Kristin. 'I didn't realise you had
company. You should've put a "Do Not Disturb" sign on
the door.'

'Um, yes. Beth, this is Matt—Matthew Lingard—my
boss,' Kristin said, in a disjointed introduction.

He nodded at the new arrival. 'Hello. I'm just leaving.
I'll see you tomorrow,' he said to Kristin, and strode out
of the room and down the stairs.

Kristin looked through the labyrinth of desks to the glass-
walled office. It stood unoccupied and empty of furniture,
ready to be painted. During her two days off, Matthew had
moved into the editor's suite which was situated off one
side of the general office. The suite consisted of a reception
area, a room for his secretary and, reached through it, his
office. Freshly carpeted in pale gold, and with gleaming

maple desks, brocade-upholstered wing chairs and paintings which Sir George had had brought in from Flytes Keep, the suite was elegant.

But Matthew's occupation of his inner sanctum meant she had yet to see him this morning. She sighed. She wanted to see him. She wanted to be with him. She wanted to hear him say how frustrated he had felt at having to leave her the previous evening.

Kristin stared blindly at a piece on alternative medicine which one of her team had written for a special healthcare feature and which she was supposed to be reading. Last night they had straightened out much of the past, yet although Matthew had forgiven her for losing him the Kinnear job he had failed to grant equal forgiveness with regard to Amanda Cousins. Indeed, he had not mentioned his relationship with the woman.

She sucked at a fingertip. This could have been an oversight or his silence might mean that, despite his attraction to *her*, he still regretted the end of the romance and found talking about it painful.

She was wondering how strong his feelings for Amanda Cousins were when the phone rang on her desk. It was Matthew's secretary, an efficient grey-haired woman whom he had inherited from *The Ambassador's* previous editor.

'The boss would like a word if you're free,' the secretary told her.

Kristin smiled. 'I'm on my way.'

'That was quick,' the woman remarked, when she arrived in her room a minute or so later. She nodded towards a brass-handled door. 'He's waiting for you.'

Kristin knocked and went straight in. Matthew was sitting behind a large green-leather-topped desk, but when he saw her he immediately stood up and strode round.

'You wanted a word,' she said, closing the door.

He grinned. 'What I really want is to tear off all your clothes and indulge in passionate sexual congress on my desk or on the floor or any damn place, but—'

He pulled her urgently into his arms and kissed her. The kiss was open-mouthed and deep. When he released her, her legs felt weak and her lips were bruised and tingling.

'No one to applaud us this—this time,' Kristin said breathily.

'No, thank the Lord, but my secretary could walk in at any moment so we'd better show some restraint,' Matthew said, and as she sat down he walked back behind his desk. 'Bill didn't turn up this morning and his wife's just rung to say he's been taken into hospital with suspected appendicitis.'

'Shame,' she said, attempting to make the mental leap from thoughts of his impassioned embrace to the lobby correspondent.

'Bill has an appointment fixed to interview Clive Chadwick at his home in Belgravia and I wondered if you'd like to take over.'

Her eyes opened wide. Clive Chadwick was a government minister and leading member of the Cabinet. Silver-haired and aristocratic, he had a stern, somewhat forbidding manner.

'Me?' Kristin protested.

'If you did a piece on him it'd make your father proud.'

'Very,' she said, 'and I appreciate the thought. But I don't know enough about politics to—'

'The interview isn't about the political scene,' he cut in, 'it's about Chadwick as a person. He comes over as a cold fish in public and the idea was that Bill'd show he has a softer, more accessible side.'

Kristin grinned. 'Well, in that case—' Rising to her feet, she went behind his desk to bend and kiss him on the lips. 'Matt, thank you.'

He put his arm around her waist, holding her near. 'More,' he said, and she laughed and kissed him again.

'When is the appointment?' she asked as she straightened.

'This afternoon at three o'clock. Chadwick's only free time was today.'

'That doesn't give me much time to read up on him and decide my approach.'

'But you think you can do it?'

Kristin squared her shoulders and flashed a look of steel. 'Watch me,' she said.

He drew her closer. 'When you come back, we'll discuss how you can thank me again.'

'Which, in translation, means?'

'We'll get together at my apartment tonight. Without an alarm clock and without your friend, Beth, and her mates.' Matthew lifted a dark brow. 'OK?'

As she looked at him, she felt a great upsurge of need and desire and...caring. 'OK,' she agreed.

'If you should meet Mrs Chadwick, what do you do?' he enquired as she walked to the door.

Kristin stopped and turned. 'No idea.'

'You ask her if she'll agree to you interviewing her for a series on politicians' wives.'

'You are so clever,' she declared, and blew him a kiss. 'Bye.'

When she returned to the newspaper office in the early evening, Kristin was smiling. Despite her declaration that she could handle the interview, as three o'clock had approached uncertainty had set in and she had become jittery. Suppose Clive Chadwick decided that in being expected to talk to her he was being short-changed? Suppose the conversation veered onto a political topic and she showed her ignorance? Suppose she made a mess of the whole thing?

But Mr Chadwick had seemed delighted that she should have replaced the lobby correspondent and immediately put her at her ease. He had introduced her to his wife, a friendly, chatty woman, and proceeded to demonstrate, by relaxed conversation, that he was 'actually a delightful and warm human being', as he had joked in an atrocious attempt at a New York accent.

Dumping her bag beside her desk, Kristin headed straight for the editor's suite. The secretary had gone, so she knocked on Matthew's door.

'Come in,' he called, and she entered to find him talking into the phone which was hooked into the curve of his neck and shoulder, while he simultaneously reworked the front page.

She waited until he had finished his call, then walked forward. 'The meeting with Clive Chadwick went wonderfully and I'm going to be able to write a really good piece,' she said. 'He gave me loads of information and some beautiful quotes.'

'Great,' Matthew said, a touch brusquely.

'Mrs Chadwick was there, a very pleasant woman,' she carried on, 'and she suggested, actually *suggested*, that I should interview her.' Kristin grinned. 'She's also offered to approach some other politicians' wives and ask if they'll speak to me, too.'

'You reckon you can fit that in together with writing about working mothers?' he enquired.

'Sorry?'

Matthew strode from behind his desk. 'While you were out this afternoon, Sir George called into the office. He wanted to tell me that he thought your working mothers' idea was a good one and said I should let you do it.'

Kristin frowned. She had been so wound up in her euphoria she had not registered his mood, but now she realised that his words had been clipped and his eyes were cold.

'How did Sir George know about the idea?' she asked.

'Because you went over my head and told him,' he said. 'But you don't do that. It isn't ethical. You seem to have thought that because I want to bed you I'd be a soft touch. But you don't ignore what I say and go to a higher authority.' He slammed a fist on the desk, making her jump. 'I won't allow it!'

'I didn't tell Sir George,' she protested.

'Then how did he get wind of it? Answer me!'

Her chin tilted. Anger burned white-hot in his eyes, but she refused to buckle and be bowed.

'I can only think that Emily must've told him,' she said slowly. 'A few days ago, she came into the office and, by chance, she saw my notes on working mothers and—'

'By chance?' Matthew gave a bark of derision. 'You didn't put them where she was bound to see them, then give her a sob story about how I was cramping your style and guess she'd report back to Daddy?'

'No!' Kristin objected.

'Yes!' he slammed back. 'You've said you want to make a name for yourself and it's clear you're prepared to trample over the rules to achieve it. Sorry, sweetheart, you do not trample over me!'

Her chin tilted further. His accusations were grossly unfair, but she had no intention of dignifying them with any further protests or attempts at explanation. If he had so little faith in her, so be it.

'Would you like me to start looking for another job?' she enquired coolly.

'I agreed you could have three months and I'll stick to it, but after that—' Matthew frowned, a nerve throbbing in his temple. 'You're hanging on by a very thin thread.'

'And you're very cynical,' Kristin declared, and, swivelling on her heel, she stalked away.

CHAPTER EIGHT

THE *piazzetta* in Portofino was quiet. Cruise-ship passengers had been ferried back to the snow-white liner which stood at anchor outside the harbour and the day-trippers had departed. In another hour or so, lights would spark on, music would softly play and diners would seep into the cafés, but in the early evening lull the village was peaceful.

Sitting at an umbrellaed table in the almost deserted square, Kristin lingered over a freshly squeezed orange juice. The young waiter who had served her—and, predictably, flirted—had described the view as *'stupenda'*. She agreed.

Clustered around a small basin of crystal blue water stood tall, narrow, intrinsically Italian houses. That they were painted in muted shades of yellow, pink and umber was, presumably, happenstance, yet a film-set designer could not have achieved a more picturesque effect. High on one of the surrounding hills, a church stood white and solid like a benevolent guardian angel.

Once a simple fishing village, Portofino had been discovered by millionaires after World War Two and become a playground for the rich. It drew visitors of many kinds. The French writer, Guy de Maupassant, had extolled its charms. Arabian princes, Greek tycoons and American movie stars tied up at the pier in their luxury yachts. The famous—and not so famous—came to wander the narrow streets—diving into the art galleries, admiring the fashions in the stylish boutiques, buying mats of the delicate local lace.

Kristin finished her drink, thanked the waiter who was topping up his tan in the still warm June sunshine and made her way across the square. Sir George's villa was tucked into a wooded cleft in a hillside on the outskirts of the village. To reach it she needed to walk first alongside the ocean, then climb up several flights of stone steps and onto a winding path.

As Emily had prophesied, the newspaper proprietor had issued an open invitation to *The Ambassador's* editors to spend a long weekend at his holiday home.

'Come whenever it suits you over the summer,' he had said. 'If I'm in residence, I shall look forward to your company. If I'm not, my staff will do their best to make sure you have a happy time. Contact my secretary and she'll arrange your travel.'

Kristin strolled past the rowing boats which swayed gently on the water. At first, she had felt disinclined to take advantage of the offer. Whilst she had yet to make an active move towards finding another job, it seemed possible that when her probationary period ended in another four weeks she would be out. This was despite the fact that Matthew had praised her Clive Chadwick profile and approved of the interviews with politicians' wives which were currently in progress.

Turning up between some houses, she started to climb the first flight of steep steps. Matthew was cool towards her now. Cool enough to keep any words between them to a minimum and strictly concerning work, though not so cool that anyone else had commented. This dismayed her—and hurt.

Whilst she accepted that he felt strongly about his word being regarded as final—as editor, it was essential he be in charge—she had been sure he must realise that his accusation of her telling tales to Sir George was untrue. Yes, she was ambitious, but her ambition had limits. It was not hell-bent and regardless. She would never even think of going behind his back.

Kristin reached a landing, stopped to catch her breath and carried on. She had thought of ringing Emily and asking her to tell Matthew the truth, but had decided against it. She was reluctant to involve the girl in their quarrel and, in turn, involve her father. Besides, she was damned if she would fight to prove her innocence to such a disbeliever. A disbeliever whom she had been beginning to care for.

'Fool,' she muttered.

The strain of seeing Matthew daily and being oh, so polite had made her change her mind about the Portofino invitation. Not only did she need a break from him, but, as someone who had contributed towards *The Ambassador's* successful rebirth, she felt she was entitled to a 'thank you' weekend. And she might as well come now, before she was told to depart.

After first making sure that Matthew had no plans to fly out to Italy in the immediate future, she had contacted Sir George's secretary.

'Next weekend? No problem,' the woman had said. 'The financial editor and the editorial writer lady, plus their spouses, are booked in and Sir George'll be there, too.'

So yesterday evening she had flown out from London to Genoa with the two couples. On their arrival at the white-walled, red-roofed villa they had found their host waiting to welcome them.

'In your rooms you'll see brochures listing places to go in the area and things to do,' he had said. 'I'll leave you to your own devices during the day, but we'll meet up in the evenings.'

Over dinner, the couples had discovered a shared eagerness to take a ferry to Santa Margherita Ligure, the nearest sizeable town, and visit a museum. They had suggested Kristin should join them, but she had refused. Although they were a pleasant quartet, they were from a different age bracket with different interests and she preferred to explore alone.

'Have you had a good time?' Sir George's housekeeper enquired, coming to greet her as she walked into the cool, marble-floored hall of the villa ten minutes later. 'I noticed you sunbathing beside the pool this morning.'

'I could've stayed there all day,' Kristin said, with a smile, 'but I decided I ought to get out and about. So this afternoon I walked across the Portofino promontory to the monastery.'

'But that must be seven or eight of your English miles,' the woman protested, raising her eyes in dramatic Italian anguish. She was short and stout, and never walked anywhere if she could help it.

'I enjoyed myself,' Kristin declared.

The path had taken her past sun-bathed olive groves, veered close to rugged cliffs and plunged down through thick pine forests. She had stopped for a while to sit in the sun and, with crickets chirruping in the background, marvel at the views.

'You didn't walk back?' the housekeeper demanded.

'No, I took the ferry.'

'Most wise. The others are having a drink on the terrace,' the woman continued. 'Would you care to join them?'

Raising her wrist, Kristin wiped away a trickle of perspiration from her brow. She was hot and her clothes were damp with sweat.

'Later,' she said, with a smile.

The wooden shutters had been closed and her room was shady. Crossing to the French windows which gave access on to a small balcony, she opened them and the shutters. Sunlight flooded in.

Her room was spacious and pretty. There were two double beds, covered with turquoise and white patterned quilts which matched the curtains. The carpet was thick and white. On one wall stood twin chests of drawers and a dressing table in pale oak, while another wall held fitted closets. The turquoise and white colour scheme was continued in the *en-suite* bathroom.

In addition to the brochures, her host had provided a tray which held everything necessary to make cups of tea or coffee, a selection of the latest best-selling paperbacks and a radio. Kristin switched it on. That morning she had found a non-stop music station and now she heard a familiar sixties tune.

Humming along, she went into the bathroom, stripped off her clothes and showered. As she dried herself, she wondered what she should wear for dinner.

Naked and combing tangles from her damp hair, Kristin wandered back into the bedroom. She could opt for her beaded tunic and Palazzo pants, though perhaps— She stopped in her tracks. She stared. There was a suitcase on the spare bed. It was not her suitcase and it had not been there before.

Her gaze swivelled around...and halted. She frowned. Someone was out on her balcony. Creeping forward to take a closer look, she saw a man in a black sports shirt and pale chinos. He was standing with his hands resting on the stone balustrade, gazing out at the scene. It was Matthew!

Kristin was so shocked that she froze, her eyes open wide. She heard a squeak of surprise and realised it must have come from her.

At the sound, Matthew turned, started and did a double-take. 'Once again we meet in a bedroom,' he said drolly, and stepped inside. Pushing his hands into the pockets of his chinos, he rested back on his heels. 'Great view,' he remarked.

'Isn't it. The way the villa's gardens blend into the hill-side which sweeps down to the sea is—' She broke off. 'You mean me.'

He nodded. 'I mean you.'

Kristin looked coolly back. Whilst her instinct was to dash frantically hither and thither, searching for something to grab up and hold in front of her, she refused to go into the headless chicken mode. Refused to give him the satisfaction of watching her panic.

'What are you doing here?' she enquired.

'You didn't expect me?' His gaze travelled slowly and

insolently down her naked body. 'I thought you were ready and waiting.'

'Think again!' she declared, and, losing her nerve, she fled into the bathroom.

She had been relaxed and carefree, Kristin thought as she wrapped a large white bath towel around her—until now. How dared Matthew arrive, out of the blue? She fastened the towel tight beneath one arm. He had no right to ruin her holiday.

'Why are you in Portofino?' she demanded, emerging again.

'I'm staying for the weekend.'

'Your secretary told me you were too busy to fly out and were leaving the trip for later,' she protested.

'That's how it seemed, but I decided that if I didn't get away from the office something was going to snap. I also felt it was time the deputy editor had a chance to take hold of the reins.'

'So you're not intending to work fourteen hours a day for the rest of your life?'

'Nope,' Matthew replied, and frowned. 'I had no idea you'd be here.'

'You knew I was having time off.'

'Yes, but I didn't realise you were coming to Italy. You never told me.'

'You never asked,' Kristin retaliated.

His frown deepened. When she had said she would like a long weekend off, he had wondered if she might be going away with the man, James, whom she had mentioned. And perhaps he had not asked questions because he had not wanted to know?

'We're not too hot on communication these days,' he observed.

'The lines of communication seem to be crossed here,' she said, 'because this is *my* room.'

'The housekeeper has just informed me that it's mine.'

'You've made a mistake.'

Matthew shook his head. 'She said Sir George had told her I was to be in the Tuscany Room and this is the Tuscany Room, according to the brass plate on the door.'

'It is, but—'

'The housekeeper also said that Sir George had arranged a pleasant surprise,' he went on thoughtfully, then he scowled. 'The pleasant surprise is sharing a room with *you*. He must've thought I'd decided to join you at the last minute and he thinks we're destined to be married, so—' He swore.

'You didn't tell him we'd called the engagement off again?' Kristin asked tartly. 'I am surprised.'

'It was an oversight. However, I shall advise the housekeeper that I feel it would be more...seemly if I had my own room.'

'You can't have your own room. There are only three guest bedrooms and they're occupied. You'll have to go to a hotel,' she declared, and shone a synthetic smile. 'A great pity, but that's life.'

'How about you going to a hotel?'

'Me?' She shook a determined head. 'I was here first.'

'I hate to pull rank, but I do have seniority.'

'You'd turf me out?' Kristin protested.

He sighed. 'No,' he said, and rubbed a pensive hand along the edge of his jaw. 'If I announce that I'd prefer to stay in a hotel—and finding a vacancy at this time of year might not be so easy—it'll raise the whole God-awful engagement fiasco again and, in Sir George's eyes, we shall both look like idiots.'

'These are difficult times,' she said thinly.

'Tell me about it. Do you want to look like an idiot?' Matthew enquired.

'No.'

'Neither do I.'

Kristin cast him a wary look. 'You're not suggesting that—that you move in here with me?'

'It'd make life simpler.'

'Maybe, but—'

'It's only for two nights.'

'Look, apart from all the other considerations, if we share a room our fellow guests'll decide that we must be—'

'Lovers?' he provided, when she hesitated.

'Yes, and word'll get back to the office.'

'Everyone at the office probably reckons that we're lovers anyway,' he pointed out.

'Well…yes.'

'There are two beds and if you promise to stay in yours and keep your hot little hands off me neither of us will come to any harm.' Matthew hoisted a brow. 'Think you can summon up the self-control?'

'A cinch,' Kristin assured him.

He grinned. 'I am tall, dark and handsome.'

'Oh, go to hell.'

'If we're supposed to be lovebirds, you'll need to cut down on the snitty language and show some affection towards me.'

'A teensy-weensy bit of affection and only when Sir George is around,' she said, then added, 'Babycakes.'

'You're getting the hang of it. So it's agreed that we share?'

Kristin frowned. Whilst she did not relish the prospect, neither did she relish the thought of having to go through an embarrassing 'the engagement's off again' rigmarole with their host. Letting the matter ride seemed far simpler. As for Matthew putting *his* hot little hands on her, now that she had become *persona non grata*, there seemed scant risk. Though if he did she could always scream.

'It is,' she said.

'Then I shall unpack,' he declared, and unlocked his case. Taking out a suit, he walked over to the closet. 'You appear to have brought a full range of outfits, as per usual,' he remarked as he looked inside. 'Though I can't see any luminous lime-green flip-flops decorated with bananas.'

'I forgot them again. Curses.'

'Do you mind if I squeeze myself a few inches of space?'

'Go ahead. I was wondering what to wear this evening,' Kristin said as he eased her hangers along the rail.

He turned to look at her. 'Have you brought the brown dress?'

To her annoyance, she felt her cheeks begin to burn. 'No.'

'Shame,' Matthew murmured. Pushing back her clothes, he came to a short white dress with a halter neck. Made from georgette, it had a floaty skirt which swirled around her legs when she walked. 'How about this?'

She nodded. It would be perfect for the warm summer's evening. 'Good choice. I'll wear it.'

'I understand we're expected down for drinks, but first I need to have a shower.'

'That's OK. I'll get dressed in here. Watch out for long hairs around the plug hole,' she told him as he headed towards the bathroom.

Matthew grimaced. 'I should've known there'd be snags,' he said.

'I didn't think he'd be able to stay away,' Sir George said, leaning across from his chair to speak in her ear. 'You're made for each other. You are,' he insisted, when Kristin gave a strained smile. 'You may have had your ups and downs, but, believe me, I know.'

'Er—yes,' she said.

After a dinner of freshly caught lobster, rice and salad, followed by a mouth-watering tiramisu, the party had moved back out onto the terrace. Sir George was seated on one side of her, while on the other Matthew chatted with their fellow guests.

Night had fallen and a crescent moon cast long white shadows across the serene black sea. In the darkness, an occasional light glimmered from houses on the hillside opposite or shone from fishing boats which trawled the ocean. The evening air carried the fragrant smell of blossoms.

When she and Matthew had first come downstairs, Kristin had been wary. Would there be comments about their relationship? Might she have to answer awkward questions? Her presumed lover might have been cool at the office, but might he intend to be warm towards her now? To touch, to cuddle? His pretence would be hard to handle.

But everything had gone smoothly, thanks to Matthew. He had deftly steered the conversation, asking about the Italian Riviera, making references to topical happenings in the world, and keeping clear of their alliance. He had been friendly towards her, but nothing more. As time had passed, she had relaxed. It was only now that anyone had made a personal remark and that had been in confidence.

'What is everyone planning to do tomorrow?' Sir George enquired, when there was a break in the conversation.

'We've all decided to take the ferry and go further down the coast to Sestri Levante,' the financial editor told him.

'A good choice,' he said. 'What about you two?'

'Pisa,' Kristin replied.

'Pisa,' Matthew declared, at the same time.

They looked at each other in surprise, then he gave an infinitesimal shrug.

'If you were intending to hire a car, don't,' Sir George said. 'My driver will be happy to take you in the minibus.'

'Thanks, but I'd like to go by train,' she said.

'We'd like to go by train,' Matthew amended.

'I've made enquiries and there's an express which leaves Santa Margherita just after eight-thirty in the morning,' Kristin went on.

'My driver will deliver you to the station,' their host proclaimed, and raised his glass. 'A toast. To Matthew, for doing such a wonderful job of relaunching *The Ambassador*. We've beaten off those cut-price promotions and circulation continues to increase at a rate which is beyond my wildest dreams.'

Everyone raised their glass. 'To Matthew,' they said in unison.

He smiled. 'Thanks, but I couldn't have done it without such a great team of writers, so—' he raised his glass to the two other editors and then to Kristin '—all my thanks to you.'

'Us both deciding we wanted to visit Pisa was quite a co-incidence,' Kristin remarked as the train drew out of Santa Margherita the next morning.

After confirming the time he would pick them up on their return, the driver had deposited them at the small station. They had bought tickets, worked out which platform they required and waited with a throng of locals and holiday-makers. When the Genoa to Pisa inter-city express arrived, they had found comfortable seats in a carriage which was not too crowded.

'A fortunate coincidence,' Matthew said.

'I suppose so, though when we arrive at Pisa we don't need to stay together.'

'Are you planning to take a look at the Leaning Tower?' he enquired.

'Naturally.'

'Then what do you intend to do, walk ten paces behind me?'

'On the contrary,' she replied smartly. 'I intend *you* to walk ten paces behind *me*.'

He shook his head. 'That'd be nuts.'

'You reckon we should sightsee in tandem?' Reaching into her bag, Kristin drew out a guide book which she had bought. 'Suits me.'

As she started to flick through pages, Matthew looked out of the window. After travelling in and out of a series of tunnels, the train had arrived beside the sea. He yawned. Although his roommate had fallen asleep within minutes last night, he had lain awake until the early hours. He had been aware of her lying in the next bed—and had wished he was lying beside her.

He frowned at the rows of bathing huts which were whizzing past in a painted blur. Red and cream ones. Blue and yellow ones. Some striped green and white. Why had he suggested that they share? He must be a masochist.

Whilst the logistics of them using bedroom and bathroom had worked smoothly—what could have felt intrusive had, in fact, felt surprisingly easy—he had been forever conscious of Kristin's proximity. Of her dresses next to his clothes in the wardrobe. Of her make-up on the bathroom shelf. Of how, twice before, they had almost made love.

He readjusted the position of his camera which sat on the table in front of them. Sharing had been an idiotic idea. OK, telling Sir George that the engagement was off *again* would have made him seem capricious and unreliable, but the pretence could not go on for ever. He should have ended it yesterday. He hadn't and so—he yawned again— he was putting himself through an exquisite kind of torture.

A few minutes later, Kristin cast a sideways glance at her companion. She had felt the sag of his shoulder against hers and now she saw that he was asleep.

She returned to reading about Pisa, though she kept a watchful eye on the passing scene. The mix of coastline and tunnels continued for a while, but eventually the track curled into the countryside. When the train stopped at Carrara, she saw yards full of huge blocks of the white marble for which the town was world-famous—though Matthew slept on.

The two hour journey was nearing its end and she was deciding she would give him a nudge, when he suddenly woke up.

'Sorry about that,' he said, sitting up straight and raking the fall of dark hair back from his brow.

'It's OK. I may've missed out on chat, but at least you didn't snore or dribble, or twitch.'

'Though you could decide to tell your *Trend* readers that I did?'

Kristin grinned. Although Jo claimed to be rigorously

searching for a replacement no one had been hired and she was still writing her column.

'Next week,' she said.

'Why didn't I keep my big mouth shut?' he complained.

Following a map in her guide book, Kristin directed them out of the railway station and across the River Arno. The historic town was a warren of narrow crowded streets which opened into wide sunny squares filled with ancient churches and palaces.

When they reached the Piazza del Duomo, their destination, they stood and stared. The three shining marble monuments of the Cathedral, Baptistery and Campanile, or Leaning Tower, rose up amidst smooth green lawns. It was a spectacular sight.

They looked at each other and shared a smile.

'I've seen photographs and TV documentaries, but the Tower's even more imposing in real life,' Matthew said.

She nodded. 'And more incredible.'

'I wonder how old the buildings are?' he said as they walked closer.

'They were started in the eleventh and twelfth centuries, and around a hundred years later were decorated with sculptures, inside and out, by Nicola Pisano and his son, Giovanni,' Kristin told him, recalling what she had read in her guide book. She grinned. 'More useless information.'

'But interesting.'

'The Leaning Tower has been closed to the public since 1990 and will be closed indefinitely,' she went on. 'For preservation and safety reasons.'

'And it leans more each year and efforts are being made to stabilise it with steel cables and such. As we can see.'

They bought tickets and joined other tourists to visit the black and white façaded Cathedral with its collection of paintings, then moved on to the Baptistery. As they walked into the huge barrel of a building, a man started to sing in a melodious baritone. Everyone stopped, listening to the voice which soared up to the dome and echoed around. And around. And around. As the last deep rich notes faded, there was silence.

'A golden moment,' Matthew said as the activity resumed.

She nodded. It was a moment which she would always remember. 'The acoustics mean that a choir singing in here can be heard twenty kilometres away.'

Placing an arm around her shoulders, he gave her a jokey shake. 'Know-all,' he said.

Kristin laughed. Perhaps it was because they were away from work, on holiday in a different country, but his coolness had been forgotten. They might not be lovers, but, for now, they were friends.

As they went outside, she indicated the camera which hung from his shoulder. 'Suppose I take a picture of you pretending to hold up the Tower?'

Matthew eyed other visitors who were striking the necessary pose and made a face. 'That is so corny.'

'Charlie would like it.'

'He'd love it, and your kid brother would love the same shot of you,' he said, grinning.

They took the photographs, then crossed to the street side of the Piazza. Here a long line of stalls sold Leaning Tower memorabilia. There were Leaning Tower T-shirts, baseball caps and videos, Leaning Tower table lamps, ashtrays and statuettes in grey, pink and lime-green plastic. After much looking and cringing, they settled for buying postcards.

'Lunchtime,' Matthew decreed, looking at his watch.

Back along a street towards the river, they found a trattoria with tables set in a shady patio full of trailing geraniums and spreading ferns. The proprietor recommended his home-made *tagliolini verdi gratinati* which, he explained with many smiles and much hand-waving, was spinach egg pasta with fine strips of ham, coated with a creamy sauce and served with a crisp cheese topping.

'For two,' Matthew said, when Kristin nodded. 'And a carafe of your Chianti Classico.'

'Sí, signor.'

As they ate the tasty food, they chatted—talking easily about other places which each of them had visited, about Charlie and her brother, about books read and films seen. There were jokes and laughter, yet the sexual pull between them manifested itself in lingering looks and the way he occasionally touched her. By the end of the meal, Kristin felt sure the café proprietor believed they were lovers.

'What did your father think about your Clive Chadwick interview?' Matthew enquired, when their plates were empty and they were sipping the remains of the wine.

'He was most impressed. He must've shown the piece to just about everyone he knows and bored them stiff with boasting. Thank you for giving me the chance to make him proud of me. There were times when it seemed as if he never, ever would be, but now—' Kristin smiled. 'Thank you,' she repeated.

'Thank you for coming to Pisa with me.' Reaching across the table, he took hold of her hand. 'I've had a good time.'

'And me,' she told him. 'And me.'

Matthew had fallen asleep with remarkable ease when they had been on the train to Pisa, Kristin recalled, but he was not asleep now. And it was long past midnight.

Because the night was warm, the French windows in their room stood ajar and the shutters were half open. Silver slivers of moonlight slanted into the room and if she looked sideways she could see the outline of his body beneath the sheet as he lay, facing away from her. She could also hear the rustle of sheets when he turned over—and he had turned over often.

After a day when the mood between them had been relaxed, her roommate was restless.

She stared up at the ceiling. Yesterday, she had felt sure she would find it difficult to sleep with him in the next bed, but the long walk in the fresh air had swiftly rendered her unconscious. Not tonight. Tonight she was wide awake and felt restless, too. Kristin frowned. Because the mood had been so relaxed, she wanted to make him understand that he had had no reason to be hostile towards her.

'With regard to me giving Emily a sob story about you cramping my style with the working mothers idea,' she began, her voice breaking determinedly into the silence. 'It's true that I—'

'Forget it,' Matthew said.

'I did tell her you weren't keen, but—'

He turned over in bed to face her. 'Go to sleep,' he instructed, frowning through the darkness, and turned back again. 'Goodnight.'

He lay still. Being with Kristin today had felt so good and so *natural*, and now the natural thing would be to make love to her. He wanted to make love and a thought niggling at the back of his mind insisted that that had been the real reason why he had suggested sharing her room. But he refused to take advantage of their situation. He did not subscribe to the view of I see, I want, I take. He was an honourable man. Dammit.

Kristin gazed at the sheeted shape of his back, then she climbed out of bed. Her nightdress was a long simple sheath of ivory satin with shoestring straps. The straps had a habit of slipping and, hooking a strap back onto her shoulder, she sat down on his bed beside him.

'I told Emily you weren't keen on the idea, but it never occurred to me that she'd tell her father. Honestly.'

'OK,' he muttered.

Leaning over him, she looked down. His voice had given nothing away and she needed to see his expression.

'Do you believe me?'

'I guess.'

'You don't sound too sure,' she protested, for there were emotions in his dark eyes which she could not read.

'I'm sure. Now go back to your bed and go to sleep,' he

commanded, his frustration moving like hot lava along his veins and making him terse.

'I've gone off the working mothers idea anyway.'

There was a great swirling of white sheet as Matthew turned over onto his back.

'Will you shut up?' he demanded, glaring up at her.

'In a minute, after I've made you understand that I never intended Emily to read my notes and—'

'I believe you.'

'Truly?'

'Cross my heart and hope to die,' he said, yanking back the sheet to make an impatient cross over his chest. 'Happy now?'

As she looked down at him, Kristin's heart started to pound. His chest was bare—bare, firm-muscled and skimmed with whorls of dark hair.

'No,' she said. 'I want you to really believe me.'

His anger died. 'I do,' he told her, and frowned. 'I think from the start I knew I was being unfair, but, well, you said I was cynical and events in the past have made me wary of ambitious women.'

'I'm not *that* ambitious,' Kristin protested. 'I'm not so ambitious it dominates everything I do.'

'I know, and I know you wouldn't trot off to Sir George or engineer things so that Emily did your dirty work for you. I know you don't play dirty, but I want to be seen as a strong editor and I'm sensitive about Sir George interfering and—' Matthew broke off. 'These are excuses. The truth is that, having lost my temper and shouted, I found it difficult to admit I'd made a mistake.'

'The proud Spanish genes kicked in?'

He grinned crookedly. 'I guess. They could be responsible for the short-fuse temper, too. I've never learned how to grovel efficiently,' he went on, 'but I apologise.'

'Your apology is accepted.'

'Thank you,' he said, and reached up to touch her cheek with gentle fingers. 'I like you.'

'I like you, too,' Kristin told him.

'Have you been looking for another job?' he enquired.

'Not yet.'

'Good,' Matthew said, 'because I want to offer you the post of features editor on a permanent basis.'

She needed to bite down on a smile. 'You're sure?'

'Cast-iron sure. You're doing a fantastic job. How about it?'

Her smile shone out. 'Yes, please.'

'You want to smother me in kisses?' he enquired.

'I'll settle for one,' Kristin said, and leaned forward and kissed him on the brow.

'That's very chaste,' he said, and paused. 'For someone who wants to climb into my bed and make wild passionate love.'

As she had deposited the kiss, the straps of her nightdress had slid from her shoulders and drooped down. She hooked them back into place.

'You reckon my straps slipping is an expression of…desire?' she enquired, a little chokily.

'No,' Matthew replied. Lifting his hands, he rubbed a thumb over each of the taut nipples which were lifting the ivory satin. 'But I reckon those are.'

'Me, too,' Kristin said, and this time her voice was husky.

He pushed his fingers into the silky strands of tawny hair at the back of her head and drew her down towards him. He kissed her for a long minute, his tongue exploring the confines of her mouth in urgent need, then he steered her back. He took a controlling breath. He would not rush.

'I want this time, our first time together, to be memorable. To be wonderful,' he said gravely.

'It will be,' Kristin murmured, thinking that what she felt for him was more than liking. Much more.

Matthew smiled. He wanted to lift her to the heights and fill her with sensations she had never felt before. He wanted to obliterate the memory of past loves and make her irredeemably *his*.

Catching hold of the narrow straps, he drew them off her shoulders and down. As the nightgown gathered in soft satin folds at her waist, he pulled in another breath. Her breasts were silvered white by the moon, their points rising pebble-hard from the dark circles of her aureoles.

He drew her closer, his mouth opening to enclose one straining rigid nipple moistly as he tenderly fingered the other.

Kristin whimpered, closing her eyes and tilting back her head. When he moved his mouth to her other breast, she whimpered again. The suck of his mouth, the touch of his fingers were swelling her breasts and creating a quicksilver ache between her thighs.

She surrendered to his caresses for delicious minutes, then she placed her hands on his shoulders and pushed away. She stood up, allowing her nightgown to shimmy down to the floor. As she stepped out of it, Matthew gazed at her in silence.

'You're exquisite,' he said.

When she lay down beside him, he was naked, too.

His hands moved over her, caressing and exploring in slow thoroughness, and then he lowered his head and began to indulge in the taste of her skin. As he moved down her body, her breathing quickened. His mouth was creating a sensual need, a need which demanded more...and more...and more.

Clasping her hands on either side of his dark head, she steered him towards her thighs and the damp secret cleft of her desire.

'Please,' she begged.

At the touch of his tongue on the sensitive flesh, she gasped.

'You taste so good,' Matthew said.

As she felt his tongue probe again, a drenching wave of emotion crashed over her, leaving her weak.

Eager to please him as he had pleased her, Kristin drew him up beside her. Teasing, she ran the tip of her tongue around the edge of his lips and kissed him deeply. Taking mock bites from his shoulders, she moved down to rub her mouth across the roughness of hair on his chest.

When she licked the brown discs of his nipples, he made a low guttural sound of satisfaction deep in his throat. Taking her time, she licked and rubbed and kissed, and eventually slithered lower down his body.

'Kris, please, yes,' he said, in a hoarse voice.

She pleasured him, tasted him. Now urgency gripped their lovemaking and need, raw driving need. Matthew moved, pinning her beneath him so that sex moved against sex with erotic friction. He had fantasised about her for so long and she was everything he wanted. More than he had ever imagined. He moved again, driving with his hips and thrusting inside her.

She trembled, gasped, cried out.

'You've been reading the Handy Guide to Multiple Orgasms,' he said softly.

Kristin drew in a ragged breath. 'It's never happened before, only with you.'

'Flatterer.'

'It's true.'

'Thank God,' he said, his voice deep with gratitude.

He thrust again, his need making him hard and fast and merciless. She clutched at his back, her fingers biting into the smooth olive skin. She wanted to laugh, she wanted to cry. She had never realised it was possible to feel like this. Never known such overpowering desire.

His thighs bucked against hers, and she was lifting, soaring into space and spinning, spinning, spinning...

Matthew smiled. He felt wonderfully drained and empty. Slowly, he recovered. Then he kissed her mouth and her shoulder and rolled off her, still smiling.

'You are one very passionate lady,' he said.

Kristin sighed a long, happy sigh. Her last climax had

fanned out through every part of her body, leaving her with a blissful leaden feeling, as if her veins were filled with honey.

'You are one very passionate man.'

Putting his arm around her, he drew her close. 'Third time lucky,' he murmured.

'But our first time together and it *was* wonderful,' she said.

'So wonderful,' he agreed.

A few minutes later, they were both asleep.

Was it obvious that they had made love last night—and again this morning? Kristin wondered as suitcases were loaded onto luggage trolleys at Genoa Airport. It could be her imagination, but some of the looks which they had received from Sir George and the other guests had seemed peculiarly *knowing*. Though their coming down to breakfast loose with love and smiling had no doubt given the game away.

She glanced at Matthew. Was he aware of the looks? Were they the reason he had become quiet during the drive to the airport, and was now thoughtful? Or had he belatedly remembered his feelings for Amanda Cousins? Might guilt be gnawing at him—and regret?

At the entrance to the Departures Hall everyone stopped and thanked Sir George for his hospitality.

'It was my pleasure,' he declared.

Waving goodbye, the two older couples set off towards the security check, but when Kristin and Matthew made to follow their host held them back. He had accompanied them to the airport because he would be catching a flight to Amsterdam some time later in the morning.

'Just wondered whether you'd settled on a wedding date?' he enquired.

Matthew tensed. He knew Sir George didn't mean any harm, but his personal relationship with Kristin was none of his business and he wished he wouldn't interfere. He wished he would not try to force things, try to force him.

'Not yet,' he said shortly.

'You should. You're so obviously in tune and this un-official engagement of yours is a—' the businessman's brow wrinkled '—feeble arrangement. Kristin deserves bet-ter. If I was you, Matt, I'd fix a date for this summer.'

He shone a taut smile. 'I don't think that is—'

'We shan't be fixing a date, ever,' Kristin declared. 'Af-ter much serious consideration, we've decided that we're both too busy to devote the proper time and attention to marriage, and we wouldn't want to end up in the divorce courts. Right?' she said to Matthew.

He frowned. 'Right.'

'So from now on we shall just be friends. Platonic friends.' She smiled at Sir George. 'Thanks again, but we must go and catch our flight. Bye.'

'Goodbye,' their host said, and waved them farewell.

'I thought that as he was applying pressure we should get rid of the engagement business for once and for all,' Kristin declared as they picked up their bags from the scan-ner conveyor and headed on towards Passport Control. 'Our time here has been fun, but it was time out. We both needed a break. However, you're up to your neck in work and so am I, and life'll be much simpler if we revert to our original working relationship.'

Slipping a hand inside his jacket, Matthew took out his passport. 'I agree,' he said.

CHAPTER NINE

EVERYTHING fitted: the main article with its two accompanying photographs, a smaller piece, the pocket cartoon and the advertisements. Kristin gave a satisfied nod and moved on to laying out the next page.

As she worked, she began to brood—yet again—about the situation with Matthew. Three days ago, she had said she wanted them to keep to a working relationship. He had not protested then and he had not protested since. Though why would he?

She frowned, recalling the spasm of irritation which had crossed his face when Sir George had asked about a wedding date. It had not been difficult to guess what he must have been thinking. That first the newspaper proprietor had pushed him into giving her her job, that, next, he had put them in the same bedroom at his villa and, finally, that he was telling him to marry her. She had understood that he would be annoyed and resentful—and so had felt compelled to make it clear that Sir George's expectations were *not* hers.

Kristin's hazel eyes clouded. Unfortunately, for her their lovemaking had heralded a new emotional intimacy. She had realised how much she cared for Matthew—and she cared deeply. She cared more than she had ever cared for any other man.

But he had once referred to 'the lust factor' and in sleeping with her he had been motivated by lust. Love had not entered his equation. Granted, they had only known each other a couple of months and love can take time to grow, but whilst he might like her he would not fall headlong in love with her—because he remained besotted with the beautiful Amanda Cousins.

So where were they going together? Nowhere. His irritation with Sir George had made that plain and, out of pride and a sense of self-preservation, she had killed both their fake engagement and any future romance stone-dead. She could not share Matthew's bed again if he still hankered after another woman. Her self-esteem would not allow it.

Kristin swung a glance along the general office to the editor's suite. As for working with him and hiding how she felt—there was a theory that if you ignored a problem for long enough it went away.

'Post,' announced a youth, arriving to hand her a wodge of envelopes.

The features section had begun to draw a regular amount of mail. Some letters asked for more information with regard to certain articles, others queried points mentioned, a comforting few were in praise. Usually the letters were addressed to the Features Editor, but this morning there was one envelope which bore her name.

Slitting it open, she took out a handwritten note. As she looked down at the signature, her eyes stretched wide in astonishment. She read the note, then grinned and held it out to Pete, who occupied the desk next door.

'Look who's written to me,' she said excitedly. 'And guess who I'm going to ring?'

Matthew put down the telephone, scribbled a quick reminder of the call, then drew the basket of post across the desk towards him. His secretary had brought it in over an hour ago, but this was the first chance he had had to look at it. Most of the mail had been opened and spread out for his attention, but on top of the pile lay a sealed envelope. Marked 'private and confidential', it bore an American stamp.

Curious, he read it first. The letter came from Thomas Kinnear. The media tycoon complimented him on the fine job he was doing with *The Ambassador*, confessed that ten years ago he had been too hasty in rejecting his talents, and said he was now writing to offer him the position of managing editor of his British newspaper group.

Matthew chuckled. He must tell Kristin.

Reaching out, he went to flick down the intercom switch to ask his secretary to ask her to come in, then had second thoughts and sat back. His instinct had been to share the news and enjoy her reaction, but he had forgotten that their relationship was now a strictly working one.

Removing his glasses, he rubbed at the bridge of his nose. The closeness which they had shared in Italy—both during the day and at night—meant that as they had travelled to the airport he had been trying to sort out his feelings. He had never felt so emotionally *moved* by a woman before, but what happened next? What did he want to happen?

Sir George's talk of marriage had intruded and taken him by surprise. And, with her announcement that she preferred them to just be friends, Kristin had surprised him, too. Shocked him. And sorely disappointed. He sank his head into his hands. She had seemed determined to end their affair before it had begun, but why?

Had he remembered her friendship with James? He did not know what—if anything—there was between the two of them, yet perhaps she had felt guilty. But would she have been so responsive to him if she loved someone else? It seemed doubtful.

So what did he do? If he continued to play along with the platonic friends idea, there was a chance she might become closer to James—or to some other man. He felt an uncharacteristic moment of stark screaming panic. Then he would have lost her by default!

He slid his spectacles back onto his nose. Kristin wasn't going to become close to anyone else, he assured himself. Not in the immediate future. She was too absorbed in establishing herself as a top-class journalist and too busy. He had time to plan a strategy. He had time to decide what he wanted to happen next.

Stretching out his hand, Matthew pressed the switch. Kristin would understand his amusement with the Kinnear offer, so he would tell her. He *needed* to share the letter with her. But he would tell her casually, in the course of discussing some newspaper business.

'Would you ask Kristin to come in, please?' he said, but a minute or so later his secretary buzzed back to say there was no response from her desk.

'Then leave it, thanks,' he instructed, and rose to his feet.

Chances were she was somewhere in the general office, or maybe in the library, so he would go and find her.

'Where's your boss?' he asked Pete, when he reached her deserted desk.

'She's out. Gone to see Gully Knox,' the young man told him.

'Gully Knox?' he protested, in alarm.

'She had a letter from the guy this morning offering an interview, so she rang and arranged to meet with him straight away, before he could change his mind. I asked her if it was such a good idea, but she reckoned she'd been offered a chance she couldn't pass up. '

'Where's she meeting him?'

'At his flat, I think.'

Matthew cursed. 'Do you know the address?'

'No, but Kristin wrote to him so it'll be in the files.'

'Find it,' he ordered. *'Now.'*

A quarter of an hour later, he was in a cab heading towards one of the rougher areas of South London. After a couple of days of hot and increasingly muggy weather, the forecast had warned of thunderstorms and the sky was slate-grey. It cast an ominous light.

Matthew urged the cab silently on. Although Pete had offered to make chase, he had said that he would go. He had insisted. An appointment had had to be cancelled, but he needed to make sure that Kristin was safe. OK, perhaps he was overreacting, but he could not sit at his desk wondering…imagining…fearing the worst.

Gully Knox was stating his views on law and order, and his views were strict. He believed in 'an eye for an eye', the liberal application of the lash, and hanging.

As he spoke—his words going into the recorder which sat on a plastic stool between them—Kristin swung a covert look around the living room. Poorly furnished with threadbare fireside chairs, a rackety dining table and limp net curtains, it was a cheerless place. She glanced out of the window. The sky had darkened and coin-sized drops of rain were beginning to batter against the glass. The gloom and rattle of the rain made her surroundings seem even starker.

She returned her gaze to the man who continued to speak. With a shaven head, sharp features and a painful-looking stud below his bottom lip, Gully Knox was a scary individual. She felt sure he knew that—and traded on it.

'When I lived in the Middle East, I went to a stoning,' he said, and proceeded to give a graphic, grisly and somewhat gleeful description of the scene.

'Did you work in the Middle East?' Kristin enquired conversationally as his reminiscence ended.

The looks he had kept slinging her said he had expected her to pale and throw up her hands in horror, but she was made of sterner stuff.

'No, I was there on my yacht. I bought it with money I received from a trust fund when I was twenty-one. My old man was a barrister—'

'I didn't know that,' she interrupted.

Before setting out, she had had a quick look through the cuttings which related to Gully Knox. She had read of him coming from a wealthy family and having an indulged childhood, but had seen nothing about a lawyer father. Yet this fact added a pertinent twist to his comments on law and order.

'He begged me not to tell anyone. Afraid of the notoriety

and didn't like the connection. But the poor old guy's just died, so—' He shrugged. 'Pa wanted me to follow him into the legal profession, but I had other ideas. I sailed off round the world, but as I reached the end of my twenties, and Thailand, I also reached the end of my money.'

'You'd been living high?'

'It was wine, women and song at every port. I sold the boat to pay off debts and became a bartender and later a bouncer at a nightclub.' His thin lips stretched into a chilling smile. 'I made a good bouncer.'

I can imagine, Kristin thought. Although, at around five feet nine, Gully Knox did not physically dominate, he was wiry. He looked as if he could floor people with a single punch—and do it happily.

'Later I hiked from Thailand down through Malaysia, mixing with some pretty low-life types,' he said, and embarked on not altogether believable claims of smuggling and drug-running.

'It's two months since I wrote to ask if you'd talk to me,' she said as he wound down. 'Why have you waited until now to reply?'

'I wasn't going to reply. After all my bad press, I swore I'd never speak to a journalist again. Then I saw you on television. I was all set to get in touch, but Pa died and I've only just got around to it.'

'Why did seeing me on television make any difference?' Kristin enquired.

Gully Knox smiled. 'You reminded me of Shirley.'

She felt the back of her neck prickle. Shirley was his first wife, who had disappeared without trace several years ago. Oh, heavens, he hadn't invited her round in order to abduct her, had he? To murder her and do away with the body?

Calm down, she told herself. Whatever else he might be, her interviewee was not stupid. He would never have written a letter which would incriminate him if she should meet with some disaster. She jumped as lightning cracked in a jagged white streak which split the dark sky. There was not going to be a disaster.

'Shirley?' she repeated.

'It's the freckles. Shirley had freckles and I like freckles. So I thought, Why not see the woman?'

'I'm pleased that you did,' Kristin said, determinedly keeping her voice cool and steady, 'because your opinions on fighting crime have been very interesting.'

'You're prettier than Shirley,' Gully Knox said, and beady black eyes moved over her. 'Got a better figure, too.'

Her thoughts went to how he had claimed that his first wife had walked out one day and never returned.

She could understand the woman's wish to get away from such a sinister character and yet, equally, she could imagine him lashing out in a fury.

She made a great display of looking at her watch. 'I must go,' she said. 'It was good of you to see me—'

'I want you to stay,' he declared.

Panic curled icy tendrils in the pit of her stomach.

'Sorry,' Kristin said, switching off the tape recorder and getting to her feet, 'but I'm running late and—'

Gully Knox rose from his chair to block her exit.

'I'm bored,' he said. 'I've tried to find a job, but no one'll employ me. Terrified I might bump them off, I dare say. Stay for a bit longer.'

She hesitated then, wary of crossing him, she sat down again.

'I'll stay for a few more minutes,' she said jauntily.

Gooseflesh was shivering her skin, but she refused to let him know that she was afraid. Why had she rushed here on her own? Kristin wondered. Because she had been so eager to write an article which would earn her Matthew's praise and admiration that she had dismissed any idea of danger, but now her haste seemed like recklessness of the first degree.

'There are plenty of ways to stop yourself from being

bored,' she declared, casting frantically around in her mind for something to say to her disconcerting companion.

'Such as?'

'You could go for walks, or jog, or take up a hobby,' she said, and heard herself waffling. 'Or—' an idea struck '—how about writing your autobiography?'

Gully Knox frowned. 'You reckon people'd want to read it?'

'I'd think it could be a bestseller. You've been to interesting places, done interesting things.' She hesitated. 'But you'd need to include a couple of chapters on your wives.'

'Sure.' He fingered the metal stud below his mouth. 'Though I'd keep everyone guessing. Any suggestions about how I should start the book?'

Kristin smiled. 'It might be a good idea to—'

She was still smiling when she walked out of the block of flats ten minutes later—smiling with a heart-hammering relief. So what if it was pouring down and she had no umbrella, and her clothes were getting wet? All that mattered was that she was alive! She had emerged unscathed, and—

Hearing the splash-splat of footsteps on the wet pavement, she looked up. Her eyes widened. Matthew was running towards her. He was soaked. His hair was plastered in a dark gleaming helmet to his head and his shirt stuck wetly to his chest. His jeans were patched with damp.

'What are you doing here?' she said, in surprise.

'You expected me to…wait for four or…five days until the…ransom note appeared?' he panted. 'I'm here because…I thought you could be…in danger.' He scanned her face and took in her air of satisfaction. 'Though obviously you…charmed the bastard. I might've guessed!'

'I didn't charm him, but what I did do is get Gully Knox to agree to give *The Ambassador* exclusive serialisation rights to his autobiography,' Kristin announced triumphantly.

Gulping in a breath, he swiped a hank of dripping hair

from his brow. 'To hell with that. I know all about where angels fear to tread and being tenacious, but are you completely irresponsible or just plain stupid? Did you never stop to think that the guy might've written suggesting you see him for some twisted reason?'

Matthew glared. He had been so wound up and to find her *smiling* overrode his relief at finding her safe and made him angry.

'When you received his letter, you should have consulted me,' he carried on. 'Did you? No. You hadn't even said you'd written to him. But Knox could've overpowered you and pressed a knife to your throat and killed you!'

'You agreed that an interview with him would be the scoop of the year and I thought you'd be pleased,' she protested, and pointed towards a bus shelter. 'Let's go in there.'

'Pleased?' he objected as she drew him under cover. 'I've been to hell and back this morning. I didn't know what I'd find when I arrived. You kidnapped or lying injured or dead. You deserve the Horatio Nelson award for turning a blind eye. I told you Knox could be violent—'

'I know,' Kristin said faintly.

'But do you bother? No, you do not! You're just a kid masquerading as a grown-up,' he stormed on. 'You shouldn't be allowed out on your own without the protection of a legal guardian! You—'

'Behaved like an idiot,' she said, and gave a choked laugh which was half a sob.

'Damn right!' Matthew slammed back, then he saw her distress. 'You were scared?'

'Terrified,' she said shakily.

He opened his arms. 'Come here,' he said, and she stepped into them. He held her close. 'Knox didn't touch you?'

'No, but when I came to leave he said he wanted me to stay and I was afraid to object in case he lost his temper and—and he reckoned I reminded him of his first wife—

and I wouldn't be surprised if he did murder her.' Kristin wound her arms around his neck. 'Thank you so much for coming to the rescue.'

Matthew rested his forehead against hers. 'I couldn't keep away,' he said wryly.

She clung to him, absorbing his comfort and his strength, then she drew back. 'Why are you so wet?'

'The cab dropped me off at the wrong block of flats and I've spent the last fifteen minutes stampeding around in the rain trying to find the right one. Taxi!' he called suddenly, waving at a solitary cab which had turned a distant corner and was heading towards them.

'That's lucky,' she said.

'Very. Whenever it rains cabs seem to suddenly disappear. Kensington,' he said to the driver, when the vehicle stopped and they climbed inside.

As they travelled back into the city, Kristin relayed Gully Knox's opinions and told him his history.

'Sounds as if you're going to write a cracker of an article,' Matthew remarked.

She grinned. 'Hope so. I'll carry on to my place and change,' she said as the cab swung into the garden square. 'I'm not too wet, my top and skirt are just a bit damp, but—'

'You can dry them in my tumble drier,' he said. 'We need to talk.'

Kristin nodded. Now that he had calmed down, he would want to warn her again, sternly and seriously, about the dangers of bowling into situations without thinking. His warning would be superfluous. She recognised that she had been far too impetuous and had learned her lesson.

Inside his apartment, Matthew took a maroon and navy striped towelling dressing gown from a hook behind his bedroom door and handed it to her.

'If you give me your damp clothes, I'll put them in the machine. I'm going to ring Pete and let him know you're OK,' he said, and disappeared.

Left alone in the bedroom, Kristin stripped down to her bra and briefs. She had gone bare-legged in the heat and she eased her feet out of her wet sandals. The dressing gown was far too big, though, being the knee-length variety, it was not too long. She tweaked and tightened it around her, then knotted the belt. She frowned. To be wearing a robe which Matthew wore was…disturbing.

'Did you speak to Pete?' she asked, finding him in the kitchen.

He nodded. 'I calmed his fears.' He took her cream top and floral skirt from her, activated the drier, then started unbuttoning his shirt. 'I need a shower,' he said, and jerked his head. 'Come along.'

'Into the bathroom?' Kristin protested. 'With you?'

'I shouldn't be away from the office for too long and if we talk while I shower it'll save time. Isn't it a bit late to become prissy?' he said, when she frowned. 'You've seen me naked before. You've slept with me and—'

'Lead the way,' she said, and followed him.

Although she tried to be unconcerned when he removed the rest of his clothes, it was impossible. Her breath caught in her throat and her pulses raced. Yes, she had slept with him, and she relived the taste of his skin, the caress of his long fingers, the feel of his body on hers.

'You want to talk about how foolish I was to dash off to see Gully Knox,' she said as he turned on the water and stepped beneath the spray. 'I acted on impulse, but I'll never act on impulse again.' Remembering how frightened she had been and thinking of the risk she had run, she took a shuddering breath. 'Ever,' she vowed.

'A wise decision,' Matthew said, standing with his back to her as he soaped himself down. 'But that isn't what I wanted to talk about. I want to talk about us.'

Her brow puckered. 'Us?' she queried.

'The reason I chased after you this morning was because—' he turned to look at her through the glass door of the shower cubicle '—I love you.'

Kristin felt her lips curl into an unstoppable smile. 'You do?'

'Yes. I know you reckoned us making love in Italy was just "fun",' he went on, half turning back and speaking over the rush of the water as he sluiced off foam, 'but it meant more than that to me. Much more. I never expected to feel like this, so intensely, so quickly, and I know the timing stinks.'

She frowned at the tall figure behind the misted glass. 'Timing?'

'Us both being so locked into *The Ambassador*. God knows, I don't want to scare you off like your last boyfriend did,' Matthew continued, 'but earlier today when I thought— Well, it concentrated the mind. It made me realise I know what I want to happen. That—' He broke off to shoot her a severe look. 'How involved are you with James?'

'I'm not.'

'Not at all?'

'No.' As he switched off the shower, Kristin took a navy bath towel from a rail and handed it to him. 'And I don't want to be.'

'Thank the Lord.' He swiftly dried his face and rubbed at his hair, then he opened the glass door. 'Will you marry me?'

Happiness spiralled inside her. She wanted to fling her arms around his neck and say, Yes, yes, *yes*! But she hesitated. She had just declared that her days of acting impulsively were over, so, instead of leaping in, she must consider all aspects of his proposal and any problems. Kristin tightened the loosening neck of the dressing gown. And the big problem was—

'What about Amanda?' she enquired.

Matthew frowned. For a moment he had thought she would give a straightforward wonderful 'yes', but she was looking solemn.

'Amanda who?' he asked, towelling himself.

'Amanda Cousins, of course. You told me how you still think about her and she—'

'When did I say that?'

'After we were in bed at Flytes Keep. You said you'd thought you were with a beautiful dark-haired girlfriend.'

'I made it up.'

'Really?'

He nodded. 'I swear.' Winding the towel around his hips, he tucked it in at the waist. 'I didn't expect to have to provide lunch and there's not much in the fridge,' he said as he abruptly remembered his duties as a host, 'but I could rustle up—'

'A cup of coffee'll do me fine,' Kristin said, thinking that there was too much of importance happening right now for her to care about food.

'I knew it was you I was...fondling,' Matthew continued as they returned to the kitchen, 'but I figured the truth wouldn't sound too good and so I concocted a story.'

'Do you still think about Amanda at other times?' she demanded.

'I never think about her.' He filled the kettle and plugged it in. 'Milk? Sugar?' he asked, taking two mugs and a jar of instant coffee granules from a cupboard.

'Milk and one sugar. Amanda told me you were broken-hearted when the two of you split up. I know it was a long time ago, but—'

He shook his head. 'When we split, I was so damn relieved. But her ego would never let her admit to that.'

'You didn't object when I told you how she'd hired a limousine,' Kristin said. 'Even though the cost was enormous.'

He rubbed at his chest, his fingers moving over the dark hair. 'You thought that meant I was still sweet on her and happy to make allowances?'

As if magnetised, she watched the circling of his fingers. 'Yes.'

'I didn't object because I'd realised that Amanda must've conned you, as she'd conned me in the past.'

'She conned you?'

Matthew nodded and made the coffee. 'Let's go and sit down,' he said, and they went through to the living room. 'When I first met Amanda,' he started to explain, 'all I could focus on were her looks.'

'She looks gorgeous.'

'She does—from the outside. But as I gradually got to know the inner person I began to realise that she could give lessons in cunning to Machiavelli. Amanda has two aims in life—to be famous and to be rich. Although I was only a deputy editor, she could see the value in having a contact at my paper and so when we were introduced at a wine bar she decided I was worth cultivating.'

Kristin looked at where he lounged in his towel at the end of the sofa. Dark spikes of hair fell over his brow, his shoulders were broad and his bare torso was muscled.

'She must've fancied you, too,' she said.

'A bit,' he said dismissively, 'but the real appeal was the clout which she believed I possessed. Clout which could have helped to advance her career.'

'Did you help?'

He nodded. 'Amanda'd just started on breakfast TV and I suggested she should be interviewed for a series the paper was doing entitled 'Bright Young Sparks'. The interview created some favourable comments which, in turn, encouraged her producer to use her more often.'

'She must've been pleased,' Kristin remarked, a touch of dryness in her voice.

'As a publicity junkie, she was thrilled to bits,' Matthew said, his tone even drier, 'but because I'd helped on that occasion she decided I must help again.' He took a swig of coffee. 'I explained the interview'd been a one-off, but she began asking me to speak to this journalist or that about her, then she moved on to making demands.'

'And you got fed up?'

'Yes, I pretty soon decided that even if I could help—
which was doubtful—I didn't feel inclined to help her. And,
finally, Amanda staged scenes where she'd tearfully accuse
me of wanting her career to fail.'

Kristin frowned. 'She was a drama queen, as you'd imagined I was?'

'Yep. By then I was not only determined that I wouldn't
be used, but I was also anxious to be rid of the woman.
You see, as well as trying to exploit my connections, she
had a nasty habit of booking us into trendy and very expensive restaurants without my knowledge.'

'Where she could see and be seen?'

'That's right. Amanda never ate much, but simply to sit
at the table cost an arm and a leg,' Matthew said pithily.
'At that point I wasn't earning too much, but, of course, I
was always left to pick up the bill. Anyhow, when she
realised I was losing interest she became peevish.'

'She expected slavish adoration?'

'Yes, and she likes to be in control. If one of her relationships ends, Amanda wants to be the one who ends it.'
He gave a twisted smile. 'I figure a guy going cool on her
was a novelty and she hated it. In an attempt to rekindle
my affection, she started turning up at the flat where I was
living or sometimes at my office. She'd go into her girly,
I'm-such-a-charmer act and generally make a nuisance of
herself.'

'Did the dark glasses slide up and down her nose in those
days?' Kristin enquired.

He grinned. 'Like a yo-yo. Knowing the woman might
arrive at any time put me on edge and made me distracted,'
he went on, his grin fading, 'which probably accounts for
why I failed to notice when your model-girl photographs
were switched. Then, stupidly, I let it drop that I'd had an
interview with Thomas Kinnear and was meeting the guy
for lunch the next day.'

'Amanda wanted to go along, too?'

'Amanda *pleaded*. She was convinced that if Kinnear

saw her he'd be so enamoured he'd offer *her* a job at one of his TV stations. When she asked the name of the restaurant I refused to tell her, but—' Matthew grimaced '—she must've quizzed someone behind my back because when I arrived she was sitting at the table.'

'Oh, joy, oh, bliss.'

'Kinnear was due at any minute, so I didn't argue because I was frightened she'd make a scene. I just banked down my anger and hoped for the best. Then you appeared and—' He shook his head in wry disbelief.

'You once said that my accusations ended your relationship with Amanda,' Kristin reminded him. 'Did she feel you'd mistreated me and so decide it was time for her to exit?'

'Lord, no! She didn't care about what I may, or may not, have done to anyone else. The only person she cared about was herself. No, after Kinnear had given me the push, I gave her the push. Up until then, I'd held back. I guess I was wary of being too critical.'

'You thought that if you were she could turn nasty and all hell might break loose?'

'You noticed that in her, too?'

She nodded. 'Yes.'

'I'd been wary,' Matthew repeated, 'but my fury with you spilled over onto her and I told her what a manipulative, grabbing, egotistical bitch I thought she was and said I never wanted to see her again.'

'You told her this at the restaurant?'

'Yes, after Kinnear had gone.'

'How did Amanda take it?'

His mouth curved. 'She had a little trouble getting her mind around the fact that I was daring to ditch her, but once it hit home she scuttled out of the place at top speed.'

'And her being so deadly ambitious made you think that I was the same?' Kristin enquired.

'I'm afraid so,' he said ruefully. 'My experience with Amanda made me ultra-suspicious of women with career goals and cynical. But you're not like her. You're kind and caring and—' He leaned forward. The dressing gown had fallen open to reveal her breasts in a white lace bra and he stroked his fingers over the smooth curves. 'And sexy and funny. And I love you.'

She smiled. She felt warm and tingly and deliciously alive. 'I love you, too,' she said.

'So, please, Kris, will you marry me? I know you were planning to wait until you were in your thirties, but—' Matthew's voice was gathering an urgency '—I can't wait that long.'

'Nor me.'

'Which means?' he demanded.

She wrapped her arms around his neck. 'It means I will marry you. Yes, yes, *yes*!' she told him, then sobered. 'What about us working together?'

'What about it? I'm happy to have my wife working alongside me and I'm sure no one at the office is going to bother. In fact, I reckon they'll all say they knew it was bound to happen.'

Kristin grimaced. 'Ad nauseam.'

'How long do you want to wait before we marry?' he enquired.

'How long do you think it takes to arrange a wedding?' she asked.

'A couple of months or so. I'd like us to have a conventional church wedding with all the trimmings because I only intend to get married once.'

'Me, too. I want to wait two months.'

Smiling, Matthew moved along the sofa to put his arm around her and draw her close. 'Two months it is,' he said, and he kissed her.

The kiss led to another, and another, and another. When he finally took his mouth from hers, they were both breathing heavily.

'You shouldn't be away from the office for too long,'

Kristin reminded him as he drew the towelling robe off her shoulders. 'And neither should I.'

'No, but there is such a thing as getting your priorities straight and before we get back there are two things which I want to do.' He pressed his lips against the upper swell of her breast. 'Can you guess the first?'

'I have a fair idea,' she said, smiling into the eyes which were sending a smouldering sexual message. 'But you want to do it properly, which means not on the sofa?'

'Correct,' he said.

In his room, Matthew dispensed with the dressing gown and her underwear, and his towel. Drawing her down with him onto the bed, he kissed her again. When his hands moved over her, her response was eager.

This time their lovemaking was different. The knowledge that they loved each other imparted a depth, a sureness, an extra joy. It gave comfort to the soul.

'I don't think I can hold out much longer,' Matthew murmured as he covered her body with his own.

'I don't want you to hold out. I want you *now*,' Kristin said, and placed her hand on his thigh.

He kissed her again. 'God Almighty, Kris, I love you so much.'

'And I love you,' she said, and lifted her hips.

Together they moved in a rhythm as old as time. A rhythm which joined. A rhythm which took…and gave. A rhythm which pounded at their hearts and tingled in their skin. A rhythm which took them to a wild, crashing shore— and delivered them into sweet dark oblivion.

'You mentioned Gully Knox writing his life story,' Matthew reminded her, 'and giving us serial rights.'

'He could change his mind and not write it, but he said that as I'd given him the idea he'd give *The Ambassador* first chance. Would you be interested?'

He nodded. 'And so would every other editor.' He

squeezed the fingers which were linked through his. 'You're a great girl.'

It was mid-afternoon and they were in a taxi, heading towards Hammersmith. Kristin was back in her tumble-dried clothes, while Matthew had changed into a clean shirt and jeans.

'By the way, Thomas Kinnear wrote to me this morning offering me a job,' he said, suddenly remembering, and he told her about it.

She grinned. 'That's one heck of a prestigious position! You thought he'd never agree to you being editor of one of his papers at your present tender age, yet he's asking you to manage several.'

'Ah, but that's because *The Ambassador* is such a hit.'

'What do you intend to do?'

Matthew was thoughtful. 'I want to stay with *The Ambassador* until its success is firmly established and Sir George is making a profit, which means for another two or three years. But I like a challenge, so I shall write back and tell Kinnear that although I'm not in the market for a change now there's a possibility I might be in the future. Would that be all right with you?'

'Perfectly.'

He grinned. 'And in two or three years you might be leaving *The Ambassador*, too. Or have already left.'

'Why would I do that?' Kristin asked, her hazel eyes shining.

'I know you care about your career, but you do want to have children?' he said, sounding suddenly anxious.

'I want to have your children,' she declared, and kissed him. 'And for me work versus motherhood isn't an issue, because when we have kids I intend to stay at home.'

'You won't mind?' he asked as the cab drew up outside the newspaper building.

'No, in my opinion being a wife and mother is a full-time occupation. Though I might just manage to squeeze in the odd freelance writing assignment,' she added.

'Like your column for *Trend*?'

She grinned. 'Could be.'

Matthew paid off the cab and they started up the steps to the entrance hall. As they neared the top, the swing doors were pushed open and Sir George walked out. He saw them, stopped and smiled.

'Oh, dear,' Kristin murmured.

Matthew looked at her. He knew what she was thinking.

'This is why there were two things which I wanted to do before we came back to the office,' he said quietly.

'I called in to see you, Matt,' the proprietor explained as they reached him. 'But you weren't here.'

'I've been getting engaged.' He grinned at Kristin. 'We've been getting engaged.'

Sir George's plump features took on a cautious slant. 'Is this a joke?' he asked.

'No. This is for real,' he said, and, raising her left hand, he displayed the diamond solitaire which they had chosen a short time earlier in a Knightsbridge jeweller's.

'What a splendid ring,' the older man said admiringly.

Matthew arched a brow. 'The lady specified a sizeable diamond.'

'When will you be getting married?'

'In a couple of months' time,' he replied.

'And you and Emily will be receiving an invitation,' Kristin said.

Sir George beamed. He hugged her and enthusiastically shook Matthew's hand. 'Congratulations! We must go and make a grand announcement,' he declared, and ushered them inside the building. 'I always knew you two were made for each other.'

Matthew wrapped his arm around the woman he loved. 'And we are,' he said, smiling into her eyes. 'We are.'

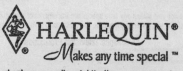

 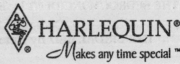

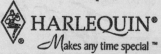

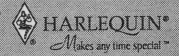

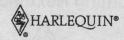

Not The Same Old Story!

 Exciting, glamorous romance stories that take readers around the world.

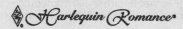 Sparkling, fresh and tender love stories that bring you pure romance.

 Bold and adventurous— Temptation is strong women, bad boys, great sex!

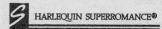 Provocative and realistic stories that celebrate life and love.

 Contemporary fairy tales—where anything is possible and where dreams come true.

 Heart-stopping, suspenseful adventures that combine the best of romance and mystery.

Humorous and romantic stories that capture the lighter side of love.

Coming Next Month

#1995 MARRIED BY CHRISTMAS Carole Mortimer
Lilli was mortified when she woke up in Patrick Devlin's bed!
He wasn't about to let her forget it, either. Patrick would
save her father's chain of hotels...if she married him—by
Christmas!

#1996 THE BRIDAL BED Helen Bianchin
(Do Not Disturb)
For her mother's wedding, Suzanne and her ex-fiancé, Sloan,
had to play the part of a happy, soon-to-marry couple! After
sharing a room—and a bed!—their pretend passion became
real...and another wedding was on the agenda!

#1997 BABY INCLUDED! Mary Lyons
(The Big Event!)
Lord Ratcliffe was delighted that Eloise had turned up at
his surprise birthday party. He'd always thought she
was an ordinary American tourist; but in fact she was an
international sex symbol...and secretly carrying his baby!

#1998 A HUSBAND'S PRICE Diana Hamilton
Six years ago when Adam and Claudia had split up, he'd left
a part of himself with her—a child. Now Adam's help comes
with a hefty price tag—that Claudia become his wife. Faced
with bankruptcy and a custody battle, Claudia has no
choice....

#1999 A NANNY FOR CHRISTMAS Sara Craven
(Nanny Wanted!)
Dominic Ashton thought Phoebe was a wonderful stand-in
mom for little Tara; it was a pity she couldn't stay longer.
But Phoebe had her reasons for going: if Dominic had
forgotten their first meeting years before, she certainly
hadn't!

#2000 MORGAN'S CHILD Anne Mather
(Harlequin Presents' 2000th title!)
Four years after the death of her husband in war-torn Africa,
Felicity Riker at last had a new man...a new life. Then she
heard that Morgan had been found *alive*...and that he was
on his was back to reclaim his long-lost wife....